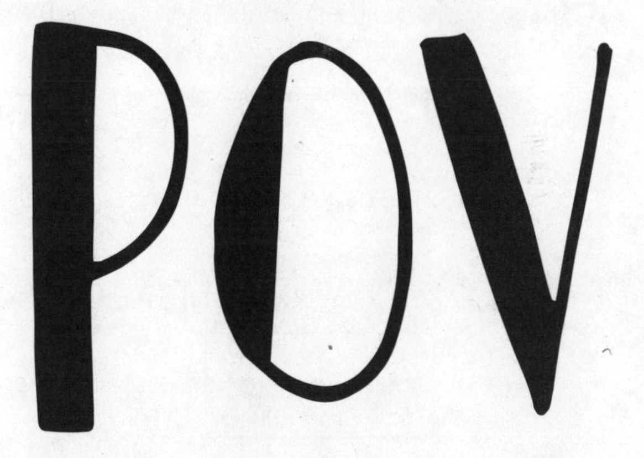

Ted Staunton

ORCA BOOK PUBLISHERS

Library and Archives Canada Cataloguing in Publication

Staunton, Ted, 1956–, author
POV / Ted Staunton.
(Orca limelights)

Issued in print and electronic formats.
ISBN 978-1-4598-1237-6 (softcover).—ISBN 978-1-4598-1238-3 (pdf).—
ISBN 978-1-4598-1239-0 (epub)

I. Title. II. Series: Orca limelights
PS8587.T334P67 2017 jC813'.54 C2017-900839-0
C2017-900840-4

First published in the United States, 2017
Library of Congress Control Number: 2017933020

Summary: In this high-interest novel for teen readers, Spencer is commissioned to create a music video for a blues-rap band.

Orca Book Publishers is dedicated to preserving the environment and has printed this book on Forest Stewardship Council® certified paper.

Orca Book Publishers gratefully acknowledges the support for its publishing programs provided by the following agencies: the Government of Canada through the Canada Book Fund and the Canada Council for the Arts, and the Province of British Columbia through the BC Arts Council and the Book Publishing Tax Credit.

Edited by Tanya Trafford
Cover photography by Shutterstock.com

ORCA BOOK PUBLISHERS
www.orcabook.com

Printed and bound in Canada.

20 19 18 17 • 4 3 2 1

For Jim M., Ethan, Rob, Matt, Will, Ian and Jim B., who have all been there and done that.

One

I'm hustling along Dundas Street in downtown Toronto, imagining everything framed as a long tracking shot. It's trickier than it sounds. Try moving and keeping your focus fixed, like a camera's, instead of letting your eyes roam all over. If you can do it, it makes you kind of dizzy. It also makes you stumble into down-low stuff you usually would see on a busy street, like small dogs and uneven pavement and panhandlers sitting on milk crates. This spices up the soundtrack, but I don't recommend it.

I angle right and into the Starbucks at Elizabeth Street. It's spring, but today is cool enough that when I push open the door, the warm air fogs up my glasses. I lose the shot entirely. I also inhale the nauseating smell of good coffee and bump into someone with a double low-fat chai soy latte. I can't see it, but these days I've got a nose that knows.

My glasses clear, and there's Scratch, sitting facing the door, back to the wall. He was sitting that way the last time we met. He could just be protecting his clothes. Scratch is a dapper guy, and spills happen. I shrug my messenger bag higher on the shoulder of my curling sweater and head over.

"Spencer O'Toole." Scratch stands and we do props, then shake hands like business guys. He's now rocking a pair of black-framed hipster specs like mine, with a white silk scarf and a spring overcoat—black, naturally—worn cape style over one of those slim-fit suits, like some French movie director from whenever. I guess you could say directing things is Scratch's line of work too.

"How are you, my man? How's Bunny? It has been a day."

It's been since Christmas, in fact, when Scratch helped me with something involving my younger brother, Bunny. I'll explain later.

"Bun's good," I say. "I'm good."

"You want a coffee?"

"No, thanks. I work in one of these places. I'm kind of off coffee. Milk too."

Scratch looks alarmed. "Why? There something wrong with—"

"Oh, no, no. The coffee's great, the milk's fresh. You just get coffee'd out, is all. Sometimes after a long shift you're wired from just smelling it."

Scratch nods. "Occupational hazards. We all have 'em." Scratch's are probably worse than mine. He sits back down. "Tell me you're not movied out too. You're doing film school?"

"Oh yeah. I'll never be movied out. I'm busy right now though, finals and everything."

"First year?"

I nod.

"Remember it well." I guess I look surprised, because he says, "Business admin and marketing. Good program. Learned to read a balance sheet." Scratch smiles. "Had to quit after second year—too much real business to run, you understand."

I nod. There are interesting movies about Scratch's business. *Boyz n the Hood*, for instance. Or maybe *Goodfellas*. Scratch sips his coffee, keeping it well away from his scarf.

"And business is why I got in touch," he continues. "I'm diversifying. Call it venture capital. Got something needs your talents. I saw your posts on YouTube. Impressive, bro."

All I've posted on YouTube lately is a four-minute school "documentary" on a local market, with lots of squawking chickens and voices in different languages. Oh, and a parody rap video I made with school friends. We green-screened a guy into a field so he was rapping to a herd of cows. That one does get funnier as the night goes on, but I don't see it jump-starting a career. "You want me to make a movie?" I say cautiously.

"A promo video," Scratch says. "For my new project. Got a band I'm managing. I need something to shop them around."

"What are they called?"

Scratch checks for eavesdroppers. He leans in. "BlueGrap."

"*BlueGrap*?"

He nods. I'm mystified. "Um, what kind of music?"

Scratch smiles. "Bluegrass rap. Down home gets down. You there? They're going to be huge."

I've never heard of bluegrass rap. But then, I'm not into music as much as movies. I could tell Scratch that banjos and beatboxes are my two least favorite musical instruments. If they're instruments at all. But I don't say that. I say, "Cool." After all, this is business.

"So here's the deal, my man," says Scratch. "I'll pay you a thousand dollars to make a music video that catches their vibe, helps me sell them. How long will it take?"

"Well, I–"

"C'mon, Spencer. I've seen you think quicker than this. And I did give you a hand last Christmas."

I fumble. "I'll have to hear the band," I say. "You know, come up with a concept."

Scratch is already standing, adjusting his coat. "So we'll say a week then."

"What? I'd need at least two. There's editing and–"

"Ten days, tops. They have a gig at the Emmett tomorrow night. Eleven o'clock. Meet and greet, and the meter's running. Concept is all yours. That's why I'm coming to you. Your vision. Loved those cows. But say goes where the money shows. I get final...cut—that's what they call it, right? Excellent. Here's my cell number. See you there. Prepare to have your world rocked."

He's out the door before I can even say I'll need to check on a few things first. Through the front window I see him take off his glasses, slip on a pair of Ray-Bans and glide away. Cut. The scene is shot: one take, and there won't be another.

Two

I head south to Queen Street and catch the 501 streetcar back to O'Toole Central. Usually I work my phone all the way home, but now there's too much to think about. Besides, I can't find anything online about bluegrass rap. This is not a good sign. Do I want to make a video for Scratch? Do I have any choice about making a video for Scratch?

I said I'd explain about Scratch. He runs the Fifteenth Street Posse. Let's call the Posse a, well, *boys' club*. Their headquarters are a gym on Fifteenth near where I go to school. The guys have names like X-Ray, Bonesaw and Cobra. Scratch and I met after Bunny accidentally got tangled up with them last summer. Now Bun's in reform school, even though nothing was really his fault. He'll be out soon. Scratch did help me with something at Christmas too. Those are both other stories and have nothing to do with this one, except that they remind me he's a guy who plays by his own rules. It can be hard to say no to Scratch.

You can understand why my parents, Deb and Jer, are not big fans of the Posse. (Neither are the cops, for that matter.) Care and discretion will be required to keep everybody happy.

On the plus side, as long as they don't find out who's paying me, Deb and Jer will be pleased I have a paying gig. Which reminds me. A thousand bucks is not Spielberg territory, but it's easily four twenty-hour weeks at Starbucks. If I trade a few shifts and power through my last school assignment, I'm sure I can get a video done in ten days. I've got a camera, and I can book school equipment and a green-screen room, so expenses will be minimal. All I need for the video is a concept. How hard can it be? Hay in the 'hood, corn in Compton, barns and bling. See? I'm there already. And I can put the video on my résumé. It would be nice to be a filmista as well as a barista.

I'm feeling positive by the time I get home. Deb is making tea in the kitchen. She has a pile of student essays beside her on the counter. My mom's main gig is proffing at York U, so this is a busy marking time for her. Jer is at the kitchen table, pecking away on his laptop. He writes the "Front Porch Farmer" column for the Parkdale *Advocate*, our local paper, when he's not baking or working on his play. He's also way more of a music guy than I am, though in a retro kind of way.

"Have you ever heard bluegrass rap?" I ask him.

Jer's eyebrows shoot up to his bandanna. "Whoa, now there's a concept. Can't say that I have, Spence. Let's see what we can find."

"There's nothing online," I say. "I checked on the way home."

"Well," Jer says, "pop music is all about hybrids. It all starts as blends of other stuff. I mean, you only have to listen to the Dead..."

I tune out briefly. Sooner or later with Jer, it gets around to the Grateful Dead. I think he's secretly stoked that he shares a first name with their lead guy, Jerry Garcia. I tune back in to hear him say, "Rap's not hugely my thing, but it could work. I can imagine the Dead trying it, Jerry on banjo—"

Deb interrupts. "Why are you asking?" She's a get-to-the point person.

"This band wants me to make a video of them. Bluegrass rap is their music." I give them the other details but carefully leave out the tiny detail about being financed by the Fifteenth Street Posse. Care and discretion, right?

"Cool," says Jer.

"Hmmm," says Deb, bobbing the tea bag in her mug. "Ten days seems awfully fast. Will you have time? How much schoolwork do you have left?"

"Just one assignment." Which I haven't started yet. "Anyway, this is related. I can use school stuff, maybe get a project credit for the video too. And I'll earn a thousand dollars, so I could trade off some Starbucks shifts if I have to."

"Does the band have the money?" Jer asks.

"I don't think that will be a problem. Anyway, I haven't committed. I'm going to see them play tomorrow night. They're at the Emmett."

"That's a whiskey bar," says Deb. "You'll get carded."

"Mom, it's also a restaurant. I'll have fries and ginger ale. It's a business meeting."

"Spencer—"

"I'll go with him," says Jer. *What?*

Before I can argue, Deb cuts in again. "What have you got the next day?"

"I'm getting on my school stuff right now." I'll take this as a win and halt the Jer invasion later. "What's for dinner?"

"Leftovers or creative curry," Jer says, shutting down his laptop. "It all depends on your point of view."

Three

We make the Emmett for ten thirty. Obviously, the Jer invasion has not been halted. For the sake of dignity and maturity (mine), I have made Jer promise to say he's my film prof, not my dad. The temperature has returned to springlike, so I've ditched the curling sweater. Jer rocks an ancient tweed sport coat that, apart from his bandanna collection and vintage Dead T-shirts, is probably his favorite anti-fashion gear. My real profs tend to dress in black, but never mind. This works as eccentric.

The room is crowded, long and narrow, with the stage at the far end. Scratch is sitting in a side booth halfway down that lets him see the door and the show. No overcoat cape tonight, but the scarf is still just so over his suit jacket.

He stands as we approach and holds out a hand to Jer. "Scratch. Thanks for coming."

I wince. Will Jer know Scratch's name from Bunny? But all Jer says as he shakes Scratch's hand is, "With a name like that, I bet you've worked a few turntables."

Scratch smiles and says, "Very perceptive."

Jer follows with some improv I should have seen coming. "Jerry Garcia, like the musician." He spreads his jacket enough to display some T-shirt. "I'm Spencer's faculty advisor." Then, "Have we met before?"

I have a minor heart stoppage as Scratch cocks an eyebrow, considering. I'd forgotten, but the answer is yes—kind of. Let's just say there was a lot going on, and they weren't officially introduced because Scratch was in the backseat of a police car at the time. I move things along. "Jer is a real music guy, so I thought he might help advise."

Jer dives right in. "Really intrigued by this fusion concept. Whose idea? What are the influences?" I have to hand it to Jer. He knows his stuff. Before I know it, he and Scratch are swapping names of vintage rappers.

On the tiny stage, BlueGrap is squeezed aboard, getting ready to start. There are four of them, three guys and a girl, all definitely older than my eighteen. The guys are in your standard assortment of cowboy shirts, flannels and tees, with scuffed Blundstones or Chuck Taylors down below. The girl is wearing a flouncy red dress and electric-blue cowboy boots. She's holding a fiddle. Next to her is a chubby guy with a banjo and a beard that's no more than a bad idea. He's also wearing one of those black Greek fisherman's hats. Next to him is a beanpole guy with big glasses and a guitar slung across his waist face up like a serving tray. In front of all of them is a little guy with a monster red lumberjack beard. He's got a tambourine in one hand and a laptop open on a stand beside him. As I watch he grabs the mike and shouts, "ALL RIGHT! We're BlueGrap, here to rock the hip-hop harvest. This is 'Lonesome Road.' Let's go!"

He punches buttons on the computer. Beats and a bass line start up. The guitar and fiddle kick into a twangy groove, slower than the bluegrass Jer sometimes puts on Sunday mornings. The guitar player is sliding some kind of little metal bar across the strings with his left hand. Mini-Lumberjack Rapper starts bouncing.

High-rise, no tar-paper shack
Banjo ain't no Marshall stack
Trade that baling wire for bling
Concrete harvest, hear me sing...

The banjo comes in as the girl lowers her fiddle and starts to sing something I may have heard on Jer's Sunday turntable. The mix isn't great. A lot of the rap gets lost in the tangle of noise. There's something about a bank robbery and a lonesome road and a rock that walks like a rolling stone. Or something. Next comes one about two Cadillacs and a girl, then a prison one that keeps looping on *razors and strings both making you sing*. All in all, it's your garden-variety assortment of thugs and hoods and rocking a Glock, with the music they play or sample or whatever, way more country. I like the girl's voice. The guitar guy with the glasses switches back and forth between electric guitar and the one slung face up that he plays with the metal bar. The banjo player grins a lot. The little guy with the beard bounces around like crazy as he raps, which is a good visual. Jer's bobbing, totally into it. They have something, but whether it's measles or a million dollars I don't know.

At the end of the set Scratch brings them over to our table. At which point there is a slight mix-up. Maybe it's because Jer right off says, "Love the Stanley Brothers sample in that last one," but BlueGrap seems to think that Jer is the man here and that I'm the guy who carries his iPad. Jer is burbling stuff like, "That dobro line is just a barbwire *snake* gliding through," and they're eating it up. The guitar player, whose name is Dev, says to me, "This guy gets it. How long have you been working for him?"

"Well, actually— "

Andy, the banjo player, interrupts. "So, Jerry, are you going to do our video?"

Jer nods at me. "Tonight I'm just grooving and advising. Spencer's the guy to talk to." He pushes his bandanna up and sips his simple malt or whatever it is.

They turn to check me out. I wouldn't describe their expressions as thrilled. Suspicious is a possible. I push up my glasses and try to sit taller.

"That's right. Um..." I've planned this—it just won't pop out. "What I'd like to do, like, is start by, ah, choosing a tune, running down a few concepts for visuals. I've got a couple of ideas myself, but leading comes from listening, you know?" That last bit, except for the *you know*, is one of Deb's lines. I wish my voice hadn't squeaked when I said it.

"*Leading*?" Max the rapper says, "It's *our* music." Uh-oh. They all nod. Grimly.

"Focusing," Jer says. "Focus is a function of leading after listening." Clearly he's been paying attention to Deb too. "Input from all. That's how directors work. Think of the theater."

More nodding, but thoughtful this time. "Exactly," I say. I'll figure out what he said later. Jer says, "So what are you guys thinking?"

It turns out they've been thinking a lot, and all about different songs. Many of their ideas involve special effects that would cost the entire project budget plus a modest five million dollars. I just nod thoughtfully and take notes on my phone. Jer has a few suggestions too. Scratch watches and sips his soda water.

Before long my phone is bulging with ideas we won't use. This is not a waste, because BlueGrap is happy. They're also expecting Jer and me to come to their rehearsal studio tomorrow night to shoot some footage and hang with them. Jer doesn't know that last part because he was in the washroom when they invited us. I'm going to leave it that way. I don't think Alfred Hitchcock started his career pretending his dad was the real director. I'm not going to either. Luckily, by the time Jer gets back the band is starting its second set. We listen a while longer, then hit the road. Jer and Scratch promise to swap some music files. I have demos of four possible video tunes on my phone. Under the music, Scratch says in my ear, "Sweet move with the prof. I'll be in touch."

I listen to the rhythmic clop of Jer's cowboy boots as we walk home. He's mellow too. "Good going, Spence. You could have fun with this. The band is great. Remember that 'Kingpin' one? Dynamite stuff." Jer's also impressed with Scratch. "I wish Bunny could meet a guy like that. It might get him motivated. I wonder if Scratch would take him on as an intern."

I don't go there. Anyway, I'm only half listening. I'm thinking hard about a killer concept for a video. If I can walk in with one tomorrow,

BlueGrap will know they're in good hands with me and forget about Jer.

I know finding the right concept could take time. Creativity evolves sometimes. For example, the rapping-to-cows video started out as rapping to penguins. But the right idea could also come in a flash. I don't have a lot of time, so I'd prefer that way. My phone buzzes. A text from Scratch:

All good. Band definitly wants Jair too. Same budget make it happen.

I may have a problem.

Four

Normally, I'd talk the Jer issue out with my friend AmberLea. AmberLea is very smart about practical stuff. She's in film school too, down in New York. But right now she's on a summer internship with a doc-film crew in Alaska, and cell coverage is spotty. I'm on my own.

Of course, the best way around the Jer problem is to come up with a great concept for the video. Normally, I'd talk about that with AmberLea too. I've seen enough music videos to know that the good ones tell a story. And the images shouldn't just match the lyrics. They should match the *mood* but show something different. A guest video director in class last year called it "parallel story."

So if we did a video for "Lonesome Road," for example, I wouldn't show a high-rise and a shack and a banjo and an amplifier, I'd show...what? A lonesome road? The rap is about traveling, but from where to where? I listen to the song three times and I still can't tell if the guy is going country to city or city to country or maybe just to the corner store. Empty highway or crowded street? You can be lonely downtown too.

Either way, lonesome roads aren't exactly cutting-edge imagery. I wonder how BlueGrap would feel about being green-screened into a field of cows.

Maybe they won't want to do "Lonesome Road." Maybe that "Kingpin" one that Jer likes will be easier to figure out. I hope so. I've had enough confusion for one night. I turn in, telling myself creative lightning will strike tomorrow.

The next day, though, I have my school project to wrap up and a five-to-nine PM Starbucks shift before my meeting with the band. I don't have time to listen to the demos again, and I have no flashes of brilliance. As I stash my green apron I know the best I can do is make up an excuse for Jer not showing and try to be on time myself. If I shoot some footage to show them I know my way around a camera, listen and nod thoughtfully, I can probably buy myself some time. Not a lot, given my deadline, but enough to figure things out.

BlueGrap has a space in a ratty old building called the Rehearsal Factory. I've been there before with friends from school. It's across the street from the Bates and Dodds funeral parlor. There's no sign—you just watch for the skinny guys with gig bags smoking out front. Sure enough, there are four of them puffing, not minding another chilly evening. I lock up my bike and take the stairs to the third floor.

The door to BlueGrap's space is open. Voices sound inside. I clear my glasses, square my shoulders and breeze through like an in-charge pro director, calling out a cheery "Hey!" Something tugs me backward. The door handle has snagged my sweater, and it's starting to unravel. I pull. This does not help, though it does increase the unraveling. I can feel the band watching as I fumble with the handle. Somehow my sleeve gets caught too. "Be right there," I chuckle over my shoulder and yank hard. The door handle is now wrapped in a cat's cradle of yarn.

How could I do this to myself? All I can do is take the sweater off. Which is trickier than it sounds, and every bit as embarrassing. My messenger bag, with camera, is slung over the side that's stuck. I figure I look like an octopus playing Twister, but I manage to escape. I leave the sweater dangling from the handle, to deal with later. "Well," I squeak casually, pulling down my shirt and pushing my glasses up from my chin, "that was fun. How's everybody?"

Judging by their looks, the answer would probably be *unamused.* "Where's Jerry?" Max the rapper has both knees bouncing as he perches on an amp.

My mind is as tangled as my sweater. I can't decide between *emergency consult with a doc crew in Alaska* or *interviewing the Pope*, so what comes out is, "Not feeling too good."

"What's wrong?" Kate asks. She's wearing retro cat-eye glasses tonight.

"Oh, just a little heart trouble."

"Wow." That's Andy, the banjo beard. Tonight he's sporting an old-fashioned bowler hat.

"So"—I try to keep it bright as I open my bag—"just us. No worries, I've brought some gear.

I'll shoot while you rehearse, show you, you know, kicking back, playing, joking..."

They look about as jokey as the crowd at my grandpa's funeral. "But then you'll give it to Jer, right?" Dev, the guitar player, shoves up his glasses. He's clearly not making this a real question.

"Goes without saying." I wish I hadn't said that, but they perk up when I do.

"Okay then," Max says, standing up to bounce some more. "See...sorry, what's your name again?"

"Spencer."

"Oh yeah, right. Anyway, Spencer, no offense, but now that we have management and we're, shall we say, *on our way*, we want the very best. Pitter patter, let's get at 'er."

"Right." I shut up and get out the camera. It's a Canon 5D. I set out the tripod and a backup memory card. This kind of stuff I do know about. BlueGrap take their places and tune up as I set the lighting. The overhead fluorescents are okay, but I supplement them with some clip lamps I find in a milk crate in the corner, to make sure the backlighting is adequate. I'm not planning to use tonight's footage, but you never can tell, so I don't want too much differential. (I'll borrow lights from school next time we do this.) Sound I'm not worrying about for now. I can blanket visuals with their music later.

We agree that they'll do each of the songs I've got on my phone three times. The first time through, I'll use the tripod and get a master shot of the whole band playing. The second time I'll have my cues so I can do zooms and close-ups of playing and singing. For the third take, I'll do handheld from different angles. Since the beats and loops are pre-programmed, they always play and sing at exactly the same tempo. That means I can edit any shots I want into the master later on, and it should all match up.

The second-last thing I do before we start is untangle my sweater so we can close the door. The last thing I do is check the camera focus.

"'Chevrolet,'" Max calls. He cues the beats, then Dev chops in on electric guitar as the bass loops begin. Max raps:

Chopped, channeled, rimmed, paneled
Low rider slow glider black widow...spi-da

Revved, stacked, heart attack
Down low, air flow, stockin' up the gun rack...

Then suddenly Kate is singing, "*Buy you a Chevrolet, gon' buy you a Chevrolet...*" and the banjo comes in. Surprises like that are why I need the master.

It's a lot of work, believe me, but it's fun. It's just after midnight by the time we start packing up. Creative lightning hasn't struck, but I feel as if I'm earning my money. I'm guessing the band does too, because they seem a bit more friendly now. This may be the time to show them I'm thinking concept too.

"So in 'Lonesome Road,'" I say casually as I collapse the tripod, "is the guy going city to country or country to city?"

Max stares and actually stops bouncing for a second. "It's pretty self-evident."

"Oh." Me and my big mouth. I'm tempted to snark back at him, *Well, it wasn't to Jer*, but I don't. Maybe it was.

"Also, the narrator is a *girl.* It's proto-feminist."

"Oh, right. I guess I got confused by the bit about shotguns and banjos—"

"Are you saying women can't fire guns or play banjo?"

"No, no! Absolutely." I babble. "I mean, especially in bluegrass rap, right? I mean, Kate's singing and playing fiddle..."

"It's a *viola,*" Kate corrects.

"And just call it fusion," orders Dev. "It's a hybrid. That's what I really like about Jerry—he got that right away."

"Recognized our samples too," Kate adds.

"Ask Jer," Max says. "I'm sure he can explain it to you."

"Hope he feels better soon," says Andy.

I try switching to a safer topic. "When can we do some exterior city shots?" We're going to need some. At least we've agreed about that.

"When's Jerry going to be ready?" asks Dev.

Before I can make something up, Andy cuts in. "Hey, we'll need some country stuff too." He's right. They look at each other. Andy says, "We're going up to my parents' summer cottage this weekend to record. There's lots of country there. Why don't you come too?"

"*Jerry* should come," Kate cuts in. "He'll be okay?"

"I guess. Sure. Cool. I'll have to trade my shift at work." I pull on my disaster of a sweater. I'm tired and wired from filming. I've also just remembered I have to "clopen" at work. I closed the coffee shop tonight, but I also open tomorrow, which means getting up at five. And I bet I'll have to do it again this week to free up the weekend too. The things I do for art—well, and money. I bet Quentin Tarantino doesn't do this, although I read somewhere that he used to work in a video store. But no video store in the world opens at five thirty in the morning. You can tell I'm not quite thinking straight, especially if I think BlueGrap would care about any of this.

"But Jer will come even if you can't?" Kate presses.

"I'll text him soon as I get home. He's probably turned in by now. Doctor's orders, you know." They don't need to know that Jer's weekend is already booked—he and Deb are going to visit Bunny. After this little chat, I'm kind of wishing my weekend was booked too. But hey, I'm a pro, right? This comes with the territory.

I'm halfway down the stairs when Max catches up with me. "Dude," he says, bouncing into step beside me, "sorry about snapping up there. I'm very protective of my vision. But listen, nice work. This is gonna be good. Hey, just a little something to run by Jerry. I think we should use 'Grits' as the video song."

I nod. "Grits" also happens to be the only song in which Max raps all the way through, with no Kate. He goes on, "And you know how I suggested lasers for it? That's probably a bit much, but you know the *diamond canyons* bit? Killer line. What if we special-effect it so the screen dissolves so I'm in a shower of diamonds? That's probably easy, right? Jer would know how to do it?"

I knew how to do cheeseball effects like that *before* I started film school. But I don't go there. "Let me run it by Jer," I say.

Five

Jer has indeed turned in when I roll into O'Toole Central. Deb is still reading. My mom is always still reading no matter what time I come in. I go upstairs and crash immediately. Next morning, after my ridiculously early shift at the coffee shop, I go down to the school to book equipment and hand in that final assignment. By the time I get home, I need a nap.

Jer, by contrast, is quite chipper. He has spread out an old sheet in the hallway, and he's scraping away at the paint on the banister as BlueGrap thumps from his laptop speakers (I sent Jer the files). He has been refinishing the stairs on and off since before Bunny and I were born. He told me once he stopped when we were little because he was worried the chemicals and paint dust might be bad for us. Lately Deb has been dropping hints that it's about time he finished.

"Hey there," he says, scraping as I yawn. "Just giving them another listen. You know, I like this stuff. How'd it go last night? Did everybody miss me?"

"Good. They asked about you."

"It's nice to be remembered. But they're okay with you now?"

"Oh, sure." I switch to telling Jer what we did. It's easier than explaining that he has been invited to the recording weekend if he recovers from his heart attack. "I think I have some pretty decent stuff, but I haven't really had a chance to look at it."

"Happy to help if I can." Jer perches his reading glasses above his bandanna. "Gotta say, the go-to track for me is still 'Kingpin.'"

"You said that the other night." I head past him to the kitchen. I need OJ.

Jer takes off his work gloves and follows me. "Lots to work with in that one. One way you could do it is by just running a stream of still photos rather than filming the band. I think Springsteen did that. And if you never see the actual members of BlueGrap, that could give them an air of mystery, you know? Sorry, I'm running on. I have to think about something while I'm scraping paint. What are *you* thinking?"

I take an extra drink of juice to delay having to answer. I was hoping Jer wouldn't ask about that one, because I haven't really listened to those lyrics and I'm too tired to fake it. Jer is waiting though, so I put the glass down and stall. "Well, not 'Grits' anyway."

It works. "Total agreement. Good call. That *diamond canyons* line is so trite. It's got bad special effects written all over it."

I nod. "I'll think more about 'Kingpin.'"

Jer pours a glass of water and drinks it. "Yeah, it's worth a listen. Hey, one more thing, if you don't mind my asking. When do you get paid for this?"

It's another good question I can't answer. I improvise. "Maybe this weekend," I say. "I'm going to Andy the banjo guy's parents' cottage to film them recording and shoot some country stuff. I can use school equipment."

This seems to work as a diversion. Jer asks where the cottage is and how I'm getting there and when, but then he says, "Sounds good, but it's Scratch you need to talk to about the money, right? Will he be there?"

It's *another* good question. I wonder if you have to pass a making-up-difficult-questions test to qualify as a parent. If I were as good at coming up with video concepts as I usually am at ducking questions, I'd rule the industry. This time he's got me. "I don't know." I'm doubting it. Scratch is definitely not a back-to-nature guy. Neither am I, for that matter.

"Well," says Jer, "I think you should straighten it out before you do any more work. Do you want me to talk to him?" He gets out the espresso maker and a saucepan for milk. My stomach lurches.

"No, that's okay. I'll text him right now. Before I take a little nap. Gotta run." I wave at the coffee fixings and back toward the stairs.

"Sorry." Jer grins, holding the bag of coffee beans. "I'm just tea'd out."

"No problem."

"Happy to watch what you've shot later, if you want," he calls after me.

"Cool."

Flaked out on my bed, staring at my vintage *O Lucky Man* movie poster, I know I'd love to have Jer straighten out the money situation with Scratch. Except there's always the danger he'll make the connection between Scratch and Bunny and the Posse, and then it will be game over. Besides, I want to do this by myself. Or have a high-powered Hollywood agent to do it for me. And I want to get an idea by myself too, not rely on Jer. There is no way I'm telling him about his weekend invite. I pick up my phone and check my messages. There's one from Scratch.

Jair sick?

I text back. **Jer resting comfortably. Going away to film on the weekend. Can I please have advance against expenses?**

I know as soon as I send it that the *Can I please* is too wussy. On the other hand, *advance against expenses* sounds professional. I have an answer back in seconds:

Expenses paid off your end. Advance when I see usable.

Contact when you get back. Clock running. Next Friday.

Six

I'm basking in warm spring Friday sunshine, waiting outside Starbucks with a mountain of gear—sleeping bag, backpack and film equipment—when Andy arrives late to pick me up. I've arranged to meet him there to avoid any embarrassing encounters at O'Toole Central, where Jer is still scraping stairs instead of resting his heart.

Fortunately, I got a little sleep last night, so I'm better able to appreciate Andy's ride, even if he is an hour late. He pulls up across the street in an old Cadillac hearse, complete with the little gray curtains and window blinds. The black body nicely sets off the white magnetic sign on the driver's door that reads, in red lettering, *HONORARY PARADE MARSHAL.*

Today Andy's headgear is a gray porkpie. The wallet chain on his belt loop droops almost to his knees. He opens the massive back door of the hearse. The space where the coffin would lie is partly filled with band gear. "Cool, huh?" He grins. "And the platform's on rollers so you can slide it all out. Hey, where's Jerry?"

"Oh, a little relapse. He's in hospital over the weekend. Just for tests."

"Wow, that's a drag. Hope he's okay."

"He'll be fine. We will too."

"He give you instructions?"

"Something like that." Andy rolls out the coffin platform, and we stow my gear in back as well. I've got the Canon and tripod, of course, three extra memory cards, a bag of extension cords and two power bars, plus four Kino Flo lights I've been allowed to borrow from school. Kino Flos are fluorescent lights that come in a box with doors you can open and close to direct the light. With a few of them I'll not only have lots of light, but I can back- and cross-light to avoid double shadows. At the last minute I pull out the camera to get a shot of the hearse. It may come in handy somehow.

Andy cackles when I tell him my plan. "For sure, man. Hey, can you get my shoes too? Check 'em out." He's wearing lace-ups with thick soles and furry black-and-white tops like a Holstein cow.

All I can say is, "Wow."

"Rockabilly or what, eh? Just got 'em. Twenty bucks in a thrift store."

"I can see why." He looks at me. "I mean, I can see why you grabbed them."

It only takes a minute or two to work out the shots. Andy pulls the hearse onto a side street where there's no traffic. I set up and get a bumper-level shot of it rolling toward me and pulling over. I pull back as the door opens, in order to get the sign, and then the shoes appear below it. We do shots from the side of the door opening, the feet appearing, the door slamming and the Holstein feet walking away.

What we'll do with this, I don't know, but Andy has fun with it. He's easy to work with too. I hope the rest of BlueGrap will get as relaxed. Maybe that's my job. How can I help them chill out? It occurs to me, as I climb into the gray-leather interior, that I've been thinking of them as one big unit. Maybe I'm going to have to sort out who's who a little more.

I keep the camera on my lap as we head off. The cottage is a couple of hours northeast of Toronto. At first we don't say much. That's okay because Andy has set his iPod on random, so music fills the space, but when we finally get rolling on the highway, Andy says, "Jer's a pretty cool guy, huh? Knows a lot about music. How long you worked with him?"

"Just this year," I lie, and keep on lying. "We don't hang together much. He's been working on this other project for a long time."

"What's it about?"

"I don't know exactly. It's called, uh, *Stairway to Heaven*."

"About Led Zeppelin?"

I shrug. "He just says he's scraping away at it. I don't know how it's going."

"He must think you're pretty good," Andy says, "if he's asked you to do this and you're just finished what, first year?"

"Yeah, I guess. But see, actually it was—"

"*That's* cool."

I think Andy missed my last words. Still, I'll take this as a win. We can get to Scratch later. To cut off the Jer talk, I lift the camera and get a traveling shot out the windshield. It's basically the effect I wanted to get the day I walked to Starbucks to meet Scratch. I wonder why it is I can make up stuff about Jer so easily, but can't come up with a video concept. Maybe I should work on getting some background on these guys.

"So has BlueGrap been together for a long time?"

"Six months. I'm really happy with it. The band was Max's idea. He knew Dev from high school, and Dev knew me from the college jazz program—"

"Jazz banjo?"

"Well, there is that, but I play other stuff too. Guitar, bass, piano, violin, some sax...It's just, bluegrass and rockabilly are really my things. Remember the shoes, man." He grins, pointing at his feet. "Anyway, Dev brought me in, and I brought in Kate 'cause I'd met her in the string section of this youth symphony we used to play in. Kate's pretty hot, huh?"

I'm not sure if he means musically hot or hot, hot. It doesn't matter, because she's both. "Yeah." I nod.

"I'd love to do a pure stringband side project with her, you know? Great player. She's real easy to work with too."

"That's a help."

Andy is a talker and doesn't seem to have a bad word to say about anyone, which is a nice change. I more or less follow the thread as he talks about the town he grew up in near the cottage, bands he's played in, how he's not crazy about city life, scraping together the rent teaching music lessons and playing spot gigs, the difference between stringband, bluegrass and newgrass music, Scruggs versus melodic banjo, and why rockabilly is so cool. He also mentions Kate a lot.

The hearse is a comfortable ride, so I don't really notice the time going by until we pull off the highway onto a road that runs through the bare springtime hills. I'd worried that "country" for these guys was going to be water skis and docks with patio furniture, not quite BlueGrap's image, but this is the real thing. We pass through a little town with a diner called the Banjo Grill (I get a shot of it), then wind up a gravel road past more fields (one with cows) to the top of a hill, where a few trees are just fuzzed with green. Andy eases over to a fence where a couple of other cars are parked.

I get out and shoot some background landscape, empty road and fields, leaving out the tipsy Steve's Marina sign hanging across the way. I can green-screen the band in later. Then I ask Andy to drive up and down the gravel road, trailing dust. I have no idea what good this will do, but if I *do* need a lonesome road, this will fit the bill. I figure you can't get much lonelier-looking than a hearse on gravel. Besides, the more I shoot, the more options I have, and I look busy and professional. My profs call this a high shooting ratio. I think of it as inspired faking, but if anybody asks, I can always say Jer told me to do it.

Seven

The rest of BlueGrap arrive not long after in a battered blue minivan. I film them pulling up. Maybe they won't ask where Jerry is. They ask where Jerry is. "Just tests in the hospital," I lie again. "He gave me instructions." That settles them for now. Andy shows off his Holstein shoes, then changes to high-tops, and we lug everything down to the dock.

It turns out we're at a river, not a lake. The cottage is on an island. And we're getting there by pontoon boat. We load up the boat and crowd on. Andy starts the motor and casts off. "Water's high this time of year," he calls over the engine as we chug across the river.

"We're on the bayouuuuuu," Max sings across the water, drumming on the railing. He's right.

The whole area looks like how I imagine some swamp down south. I get shots of the band with the riverbank behind them. As a bonus I even capture a boarded-up cabin behind some tumbling trees. Very authentic-looking, I figure.

Thanks to the spring runoff, the island is partly underwater. The cottage itself is a quite cool green geodesic dome on stilts. There are also three little cabins on a platform behind it. Andy eases through the trees and right up to the platform to tie off. "In summer this is the front lawn," he says, laughing.

We climb off and check things out. The living space inside the dome has a kitchen area, with couches facing a big window onto the river and lots of space for the band to set up. Two of the little cabins are for sleeping, and the third is the washroom. BlueGrap start on their gear. I film them unloading. None of us have a good time with this. The warmth and water have brought out the mosquitoes. I'm filming and swatting, BlueGrap is hauling and swatting. I'm shooting from the pontoon boat as Max walks toward me to fetch more gear, Dev and Kate close behind. He swerves, bats at a mosquito and vanishes.

There's a shout and a splash arcs up. He's literally missed the boat.

Everyone rushes over. Max is soaked and already shivering, standing in water up to his waist. "It's cold, it's cold, get me outta here!"

"At least you weren't carrying my guitar," Dev says.

You know how your parents always insist you take clean socks or a sweater or whatever? Now I know why. Max hasn't brought spare anything. We wrap him in a big towel from the cottage, trek back across the river and drive down to the laundromat in town, where we toss his stuff in a dryer. As Max huddles in his towel, Andy gets me to show everyone the shots of the hearse and his shoes. "Wicked or what, huh?" He looks at Kate.

She smiles and shrugs. "Yeah, but how can we use it?"

Max pipes up from beneath his towel. "'Grits,' you guys. Remember that line *walk concrete acres in my shoes*?" He wiggles his bare toes at everyone.

"Or in 'Chevrolet,'" Dev counters, "where Kate sings *won't walk that sad, sad road*."

"What? That doesn't fit!" Max waves his arms. The towel droops. He has a tattoo of a sinking ship on his chest. "They're not even girls' shoes."

"Sure it fits," Dev argues. "The point is, she's with—well, us."

"You can't walk sad in shoes like those," Andy says.

"But that's not the shot!"

"First, it could be ironic. Second, it doesn't have to be *this* shot. This is just a starter. You know, like doing a lyric rewrite."

"You know I don't do rewrites, Dev," says Max. "Neither does Neil Young. My best stuff is all stream of *c*."

Andy checks the time left on the dryer. I keep my mouth shut. I'm not even sure what they're talking about, but I can tell this is about more than a few seconds of video footage. What I'd really like to do right now is film it all. Luckily, Andy comes up with an idea. While Max's stuff keeps on tumbling, we head out into the sunshine.

It doesn't take long to work out the shots. A few locals watch us, but no one interrupts. Max seems quite happy to be bopping around in a towel. I set up on the sidewalk, at bumper level again, facing the street. Andy rolls the hearse up, stopping so the passenger door is right in front of me. There are a few dead seconds of hearse as they get ready on the far side (hey, *hearse, dead...* I'm better at this than I thought), but I can edit those out. Then the door swings open and feet appear, as one after another they climb through the hearse from the street side, step out and stride away as if they've all been sitting in some monster-sized passenger seat. Then we do shots of them in the same order, walking toward the camera and away from it. We need a few takes to get it right, especially stopping the hearse in exactly the right spot, but it makes for a good shot, particularly when you see Max's bare feet with a blue towel hanging above his ankles. You won't hear him swearing as he walks barefoot on the pavement either when we add the music. What music we'll add and where they're walking to and if I even use this—well, that's for later. The main thing for now is, BlueGrap is liking what they see. By the time Max's clothes are dry, my cred has gone up a notch or two, and everybody seems happy again.

Eight

At least, I think my cred has gone up a notch or two. Back at the geodesic dome it's time to think about dinner. Andy fires up the barbecue, beers get passed around, and Little Feat's *Sailin' Shoes* goes on the sound system. I know the album from O'Toole Central. I sip at my beer and try to blend into the background, camera ready. *Be the wallpaper*, one of my profs likes to say.

Kate sinks down in the beanbag chair next to mine. The cat-eye glasses are gone. "That was a good idea about the feet," she says, smiling.

"Thanks, but really, you guys did that."

"Well, it started with that shot you did with Andy—anyway, I think it would work great with 'Chevrolet.' I mean, show it to Jerry, see what he thinks."

"'Grits,'" Max calls from across the room.

Kate ignores him. "Too bad he can't be here. I hope he's okay. But he sent instructions, right?"

"So, Spencer," Max says, bouncing and chopping onions. "How long have you been working with Jer?"

Haven't I already answered this one? I go for a joke. "All my life. It feels like."

"No, really. Is this your first project?"

"First with Jer, but I've been doing shoots since I was about twelve. The first time I crewed was for a doc about the War of 1812." I don't mention that it was an accident or that I also played Laura Secord. "Right now I'm doing a project about my grandfather. Jer's advising."

"How old are you now?" Kate asks.

"Nineteen." This will be true fairly soon. Well, in eight months.

"You don't look it."

"I get that a lot."

"See?" Andy says, prying hamburger buns apart. He's now wearing a high-crowned Harley-Davidson trucker cap. "I told you. First year and already Jerry's using him. Did you know Jerry's doing a movie about Led Zeppelin?"

"*Really*? I *love* Led Zep. I gotta check out his stuff online." Max waves his knife. "What's Jer's last name?"

"McLean," I say, which is Deb's family name. Instantly I remember that's wrong. "I mean"—I fumble—"his real name is Garcia, but he goes by McLean so he doesn't get confused with the other Jerry Garcia. But there's no point checking online. He never ever posts anything. Doesn't do social media." This all tumbles out at the speed Max fell into the water. Luckily, they don't seem to notice. Instead, Dev says, "Cool, I understand. That way no one rips you off. So does Jerry work with Scratch a lot?"

I decide to try one more time. "Actually, Scratch contacted *me*. I brought Jerry in."

"How does Scratch know you?"

"My brother. They met at a gym. He's away at school now." I try to change the subject. "How did you guys meet Scratch?"

"We were busking downtown. He was walking by and dug the groove. Gave us his card and said to let him know our next gig. So we did." Dev roots the card out of his wallet and passes it to me. It's shiny black with silver lettering. *Done from Scratch.* There's an email and a phone number and the address of a fancy bank tower downtown. I know from experience that Scratch has different business cards for different occasions. Also that his office is in the Fifteenth Street gym, if it's anywhere. "Have you been to his office?"

"Naw, we meet at the Emmett or the studio. Scratch says the biggest mistake you can make in the music business is to have your ears in the office instead of the street."

"He should know," Max says. "He's worked with some big names—Drake, Lamar, Kanye. Did you know he discovered the Weeknd?"

I'm doubting this big-time. Scratch is into lots of things, but T-Bird and Ripple are the biggest names I've ever heard him mention. What kind of line has Scratch been feeding these people? Then again, who am I to talk? Maybe I won't tell them that Scratch isn't quite what he seems. Who is? Not BlueGrap. They're middle-class Toronto kids like me, playing American music from the ghettos and the South. What kind of line have they been feeding *him*?

I don't say any of that. What I say is, "Wow." They've opened their second and third rounds of beer by now, so my short answer seems to be enough. Dev is asking Max what desserts he brought from the bakery he works in. Max is teasing Dev that they're too good for the restaurant where Dev is a waiter. The music has changed. First N.W.A. and now the Jayhawks, another staple at O'Toole Central. Andy is picking along on an acoustic guitar. I think he's even better on it than he is on banjo. Kate looks out at the river and says this is so much better than doing data input at her day job. We're practically one big happy family. Maybe this is the time. I struggle to sit up in my beanbag chair. "So tell me what song you think we should build the video around," I say.

"'Grits,'" calls Max instantly.

"'Chevrolet.'" That's Dev and Kate, overlapping him.

"Aw, man," Max complains.

I say, "Andy?"

He shrugs and keeps picking. Then he stops and says, "When you get down to it, they're all kind of about traveling, changes, you know?

Moving on." His face reddens, and he laughs and rips out a lightning guitar lick as a song ends. "Love to have the shoes in there though. What do you think, Spencer?"

Is this a breakthrough moment? It has to be. He's not asking what Jer thinks, but what I think. But what *do* I think? I still don't know. I spin. "Andy's right—the songs all have similar themes, so the question is really which one has the best visuals as well as sound to rep you guys."

"'Grits,'" Max says again.

"Can't be," Kate insists. "Too much rap and no backing vocals. They're a big part of our sound. I still vote 'Chevrolet.'"

"The visuals would be tough," Andy points out. "Gotta have the car, at least."

"We use the hearse," Dev says.

They start chewing that over. Is a Cadillac hearse technically a Chevrolet? Then Max says that "Chevrolet" has too much viola. Kate begins to argue back. They're getting nowhere. I can see this is the time to focus them, to lead after listening. But where do I lead them? All I've got is Jer's suggestion. I cut in. "What about 'Kingpin'?"

Max, Dev and Kate all frown. *Oops.*

"That's a B side," says Kate.

"Well, we're recording it tonight." Andy's voice fills the sudden silence. "Let's see how it goes." He puts down the guitar. "And let's get those burgers on."

Nine

I get my first real idea, or part of it anyway, around two in the morning. It's been a long night of recording for all of us. I've been having trouble with shadows, moving the Kino Flos, and the band has been having trouble with everything. Dev and Kate have gone outside for a break. Andy mans the recording equipment, and Max tweaks his vocal:

Compton to South Caroline
Harlan County in the mine
Different picks and different rocks
Different rap but money talks
Gotta get, gotta get, gotta get up and be the Kingpin
Nothin' in the valley

Kingpin
Rhymin' in the alley
Kingpin
Diamonds out of coal
Kingpin
Down the rabbit hole....

The *Kingpin* lines are sung in harmony by the whole band. They're just fine. Max, though, keeps changing his own vocals. For a guy who doesn't rewrite lyrics, he sure is picky about how he raps them. He's been fiddling with how he does bits and pieces of this first verse for an hour at least. Right now he's listening as Andy demonstrates board effects that will alter Max's voice on *hole* to either an echo like he's in the Grand Canyon, an acceleration like he's being sucked into a vacuum cleaner, or one that bottoms out like he's falling down a well. Max considers these with the intensity I'd reserve for programming a zombie film festival or choosing when to declare war on an evil intergalactic empire. Slouching in my beanbag chair, I get a great profile close-up of Max as he bites his lip, considering, headphones askew and one hand stroking his beard. I've been trying to get lots of close-ups tonight.

Andy goes outside for a smoke. Max keeps punching buttons and listening. I want to tell him to go with the falling-down-a-well voice, but I'm being wallpaper. It's surprising how little attention they've paid to me scurrying around them once they got busy. Now, though, I just want to go to bed. Those clopens have finally caught up to me. Maybe it's because I'm so tired that I'm half dreaming, but I suddenly flash on a visual. It's nowhere near a whole video, but it's a great image, and that's a start. We can green-screen it, and I can do an edit.

I sit up as Andy bustles back inside. Max looks up, annoyed. Andy doesn't notice. He's kind of red in the face, looking a little annoyed himself. "I've had it for tonight," he snaps, yanking his sleeping bag out of a pile. "Shut 'er down when you're done, okay?" He stomps out, and a second later a light flares in one of the little cabins.

Kate and Dev come back inside together, looking a little rumpled. Dev is putting his glasses on. They're red in the face too, but looking more embarrassed than annoyed. They grab their sleeping bags too, saying something to Max, who waves them off. I don't hear what they say. I'm still seeing that image. I don't have the connections, but I know our song is going to be "Kingpin" and that I have to lead BlueGrap there. Right now, though, I'm going to follow the others' lead and sack out. Max is still at the board as I roll out my sleeping bag and fall asleep on the couch.

Next morning (or maybe it's early afternoon) the sky is sunny, but the mood is not. I'm not sure what's gone wrong, but brunch at the Banjo is weird. I don't think they have hangovers, but Andy is quieter than usual, Kate and Dev are both faster on the draw, and Max's knees are going like jackrabbits. On the plus side, my idea still seems good, but this is definitely not the moment to share it. The general grumpiness hasn't been helped by the review of some of the footage I shot. Noses looked funny. Someone's tongue was sticking out. Kate said her butt looked three miles wide. It didn't.

"Hey," I tell them, "we won't use most of this. It's a huge shooting ratio. Don't worry. Just remember: if you look bad, I look bad." I'm proud of thinking up that last bit.

Kate is not impressed. "God, I wish Jerry was here." See what I mean about not leading them right now?

Meanwhile, Dev is getting on Max for dithering so long over his vocal. "We've got another song to record!"

Max argues back, toes tapping and one hand drumming on the table, while he eats bacon with the other. "We want 'Kingpin' to be perfect!"

Andy sips his coffee. He looks as if he'd rather be picking his banjo.

I myself am quite hungry. I think having an idea has given me an appetite. I'm also starting to realize how much of this project is not about making a video at all. It's about keeping—or getting—everybody working together. It's amazing. What I really am is a camp counselor with a camera. I have to get everyone on board and paddling the canoe in the same direction.

My ringtone sounds. It's a text from Deb. **All goes well? Clean socks.**

I text back, **All good. Glad I brought them. Focus is...**

My phone buzzes again. It's Jer this time. **Hoping they're rocking Kingpin.**

And in a flash, I see how to get them all in the canoe. It may not be ethical, but hey, every camp counselor I ever met loved dirty tricks.

"Message from Jer." I interrupt the bickering and lay my phone on the table. They all lean in to see the text.

"Jer really wants 'Kingpin'?" Max asks.

"That's why I mentioned it," I say. "He sent me a text earlier this morning. He's been listening to that one over and over, and he has a concept."

"What is it?"

"Why didn't you *tell* us?"

"He hasn't told me yet. All I know is we have to nail this shoot and we'll be green-screening early next week. Jer will be there."

Ten

The canoe turns in the right direction. By the time we leave early Sunday afternoon, BlueGrap have "Kingpin" and "Chevrolet" recorded, and I've shot all kinds of stuff, from washing dishes to snoozing to tap-dancing. Like I said, it's a high shooting ratio.

Andy drops me and the equipment off at school. Even on Sunday there are people hanging around the film department. I've got one of the green-screening rooms booked for Tuesday. Now I return the Kino Flos and dump the stuff from the camera's memory cards onto my laptop hard drive. I watch some of the footage. Naturally, there are the usual glitches—out-of-focus shots, shadows, background thingies sprouting from heads, visible nose boogers, etcetera. It's surprising how contorted people's faces get when they sing. Maybe that's partly why videos are lip-synched. Still, there are bits that look great.

Even though I still don't have a storyline, and I haven't shot my cool idea, I've got enough to patch together a sample of my work to show Scratch and get my advance. I think I deserve one by now.

I text him. We agree to meet after I finish my shift tomorrow, at the McDonald's near Fifteenth Street. Then I hop the streetcar to O'Toole Central. I'm tired again, and I have to open in the morning. Are Hollywood hours like these?

Deb and Jer are back from visiting Bunny. They're sitting in the front-porch sunshine, having tea. We talk about how my brother is doing. He only has a couple more months to go. "And your weekend?" asks Deb.

"It was good." I give them an edited version on the general principle that it's bad for parents to know too much about anything. I do tell them how hard it has been to steer the canoe.

Deb laughs. "You should try it with an academic committee sometime."

"Or a theater collective," Jer adds.

"But that's why you're directing," says Deb. "Focus is a function—"

"Of leading after listening," I finish for her. "I listen. I even have an idea. But now I have to get them to listen to me." I leave out the trick I played in the restaurant.

"Whatever works," says Jer, validating me without knowing it. "All's fair in love, war and directing. Lies, bribes, favoritism, threats. Fear is always good."

Deb laughs again and swats Jer's knee. "Your dad might have a point. Read some Machiavelli."

"As soon as I finish *The Big Sleep*," I promise, thinking Machiavelli sounds suspiciously like a specialty coffee. *The Big Sleep* was Jer's suggestion. Actually, it's quite good. And it was made into a movie.

"Show us a little bit of what you've got," Jer coaxes. We move into the shade, and I run what I've sampled for Scratch on my laptop, with "Kingpin" for the soundtrack. There are bits of the country road, the boat ride and the band recording, finishing with a shot of the Holstein shoes. The rest I've saved but left out. "Hey, you went with 'Kingpin.' Good call." Jer smiles.

"You show how the recording comes together, but I think it needs to tell a story that plays off the song somehow." Deb nods.

Well, we're all agreed about that. "That's coming," I say. "There are city locations to shoot and some green-screening." Okay, so my idea is not yet a story, but maybe it will lead to one. I keep it vague. "Andy the banjo guy says the songs are all about traveling. I'm thinking something about them going to the country to record and then they come to the city."

"That's a good start," Jer says. "'Kingpin' is for sure about moving between the two. But why are they coming to the city? Fame and fortune? Fleeing angry farmers?"

Two more additions to his string of good questions. "Not sure yet," I admit, then fake it a little. "They can't make up their minds."

"How long did you say you have to get this done?" *Another* good question. How can parents do this?

"I have to turn in a rough cut Friday."

Jer whistles.

"Andy has the hearse and the shoes?" Deb asks.

I nod. "The hat guy."

Jer chuckles. "Rockabilly or what? You know who would have loved those shoes? Let me show you." He hustles into the house and comes back with a hefty book. It's volume one of an Elvis bio he's raved about before. Jer flips through and shows us different photos of young Elvis wearing black-and-white shoes something like Andy's. "See?" he says. "Your man Andy's in good company. The King would have loved those kicks. He was big on Cadillacs too."

"The King?"

"Elvis's nickname. You know that. Haven't you read this yet? I thought I'd recommended it before."

He passes me the book. You could use it for weight lifting. "Right after Macchiato," I say. I have to have this done in a week, not a semester.

"Get them jumping up and down when you green-screen," Jer advises. "Ever seen those Richard Avedon photos where he gets his portrait subjects to jump first, just to loosen up? Jumping's always good." I'm closing the laptop. "And that bit where the little guy is banging the tambourine? You know what could be cool there? Maybe you could get this on Tuesday. I read it somewhere: coat the tambourine head with milk so it flies off in slo-mo when he hits it. That would would be a cool effect. And..."

"Thanks," I call as I head inside, Elvis in hand. "You've given me a bunch of great ideas." And he has. He really has. "What time is dinner?"

Eleven

"Promising." Scratch nods and takes out his earbuds. "I see why Jer likes it." I shut down the file on my laptop.

Scratch leans well over the table before taking a bite of his Big Mac. Today he's sporting a tan suit, worn sockless with orange brogues and a yellow pocket square. We're sitting away from the windows, and Scratch, naturally, is facing the door, back to the wall. "I knew you could get your hustle on, my man. But"—he gives me a deadpan stare through his hipster glasses—"it's just a start. I came to you for that special vision. How you going to make it special, tie it all up in a bow?"

I'm prepared for this. After talking with my folks, I've added to my idea, but it's almost impossible to explain. The only way I can convey it properly is to just do it, so what I say to Scratch is, "It's a journey motif. City and country. The *mise-en-scène* changes, and so will they." Scratch frowns. *Mise-en-scène* was a bad word choice for my current audience, but it's my favorite phrase from first year.

"Change how?" Scratch persists. "What's the hook? We need a hook, some special effects. The clock is ticking."

"Don't worry. Jer has one," I lie. After my conversation on the front porch yesterday, I now officially have no conscience about this stuff. All's fair. I go with what works and take it right over the top. "He hasn't told me yet. Just following instructions. That's his style."

Scratch eyes me. "But Jer knows?"

"Jer knows. You heard about his Led Zeppelin project?"

"Thought that little Max dude said U2."

"Whatever. The point is, they trust him. They're not asking what the hook is."

Scratch chews this over with some fries.

"And," I go on, "Jer said to get the advance because we're going to have expenses finishing up this week. And you said we'd get the advance when you saw usable footage." I nod at my laptop. "So..." My bullroar generator is running out of power.

Scratch takes a napkin from the pile he stacked on his tray and wipes his fingers. Then he folds his arms under that perfect yellow pocket square and stares at me. He has an impressive stare. "How's Jer's health?" Scratch's tone suggests he could make it get a lot worse.

"Maybe doing better. I'm going to see him later this aft. I think he's Skyping with Bono about now."

"Thought you said Led Zeppelin."

"Isn't he in Led Zeppelin? One of those old band guys."

"He putting them ahead of us?" I hear icicles forming on the words.

"No, no! Jer's all in. It was the only time he could talk with them. The time difference between here and England, right? Otherwise he'd be sitting here with us."

Scratch zaps me with another ten seconds of full-on stare. Then he sighs and slips a checkbook and sleek silver pen out of his jacket. "Payable to?" he asks, beginning to fill it in.

I spell out my name.

"Not Jer?"

"He's advising. I'll pay him."

Scratch finishes, tears the check from the book and starts to write another, without looking up. "Here's how it goes down. Ten days was the deal. That's Friday. I believe in you and Jer so much that I'm gonna give you the final check now too, postdated for Friday. I'm trusting you to be done by the day you can cash this." He looks up at me over his glasses. "I'm walking the tightrope here. I'm the one who stands to lose. But you're Bunny's brother, so I know you won't let me down. Fair deal?"

"Sure. Fair deal. That's great. Thanks, Scratch."

He scribbles his signature and passes me the checks. *One-Five Enterprises*, they say. Scratch's signature is even more difficult to read than mine. The check on top is for nine hundred dollars and dated for Friday. That means—

"The advance is only a hundred dollars? I've got expenses."

"Hey, I got lunch, didn't I?" Scratch sounds offended. He stands, buttoning his jacket. "You can make it till Friday. Don't tell me ol' Jer doesn't have some deep pockets, hanging with those famous dudes." He picks up his phone. "That Andy, his ride really a hearse?"

"Uh-huh. You can store all kinds of gear in the back."

Scratch shakes his head. "My only ride in a hearse will be my last one. Till then I'm aiming for Audi. Musicians are weird, Spencer O." With that, Scratch makes his exit.

I pick at my fries and wish I'd ordered another cheeseburger. It isn't until Scratch is gone that I notice the hundred-dollar advance is also post-dated for Friday. I sigh, then put them both in my pocket. I pack up my laptop, gather my camera bag and bike helmet, and take both our trays to the waste station. I'm glad Starbucks direct deposited my pay. I'm going to need money for my next stop.

Twelve

At the costume-rental shop I cheap out and only get two costumes, a medium and a small. It'll be a tight squeeze for Andy, but a budget is a budget.

It's late afternoon by the time I get back to O'Toole Central. I've stopped off along the way to shoot a couple of random city streets, including ours. Jer is making progress on the stairs. The railing looks close to done, and a couple more banisters have been stripped. A Grateful Dead concert recording on his computer provides the soundtrack as he works.

The music makes a weird kind of sense right now. Jer's face and hair and beard are flecked with speckles of white paint, making him look like a spooky version of his Dead (and dead) hero,

Jerry Garcia. Jer would be pleased if he knew. Before I can tell him, though, he nods at the bag I'm holding. "Whatcha got?"

"Costumes. I'm green-screening the band tomorrow."

"Let's see." He takes the bag and pulls out a costume. "What the—*Elvis*?"

"Yeah. Remember how you said Elvis would've liked Andy's shoes? And that he was the King?"

"Whoa," says Jer. "As in '*King*pin'?"

"Exactly. Why not?" I say. I'm a teeny bit miffed he got it before I could tell him. But maybe that means it's a good idea.

"No, I love it, but what are you going to do with these?"

"It's difficult to explain."

"Will the band get it? I guess your guy Andy will like it, for one."

"It'll be easy, if you'll help me with something. Say, did you know you look kind of like a ghosty Jerry Garcia right now?"

Jer grins. He turns and looks in the hallway mirror. "Hey, you're right...minus a hundred pounds, I'm pleased to say." He goes to brush the specks out of his hair.

"No, don't," I say. "It's perfect for what you can help me with."

The afternoon is overcast, so the natural light from the bedroom window upstairs adds to Jer's eerie paleness. I position him in the armchair and set the Canon on its tripod. I'm breaking out a wireless microphone when I think, What am I doing? I'm getting too high-tech for my own good. The more basic this is, the better. And the faster the better too, before Jer starts asking too many questions. I get out my phone instead.

"What are we doing?" Jer asks.

"I need you to record a message to BlueGrap. It would mean a lot to them."

"Really? That's nice. They were fun kids. They've been thinking of me?"

"They sure have."

"Okay, let me just get cleaned up first."

"No! Listen, they like you because they say you're, um...authentic. Hands on, you know?"

"Well, this doesn't look *authentic.* You said I look like a ghost."

"I was just kidding. You look great."

"No, I don't. They'll think I'm sick."

"That's okay."

"No, it's not."

"Yeah, it is. I told them you weren't feeling so good."

Jer makes a face. "What did you do that for?"

Oh man. I say it fast, as if that's going to help. "So they wouldn't expect you at green-screening or at the cottage."

"They wanted me at the cottage? Why didn't you tell me? And they're expecting me tomorrow? Cool! Why?"

See? This is why you censor stuff you tell parents. You let one little thing slip, and they're all over it. It's too late now. "They kind of think you're in charge of making the video."

"Me? I thought I was just your helpful faculty advisor."

"I guess you were more convincing than I was."

"Geez, sorry, Spence. I was just trying to help." He doesn't look sorry.

"That's okay."

"Would it be better if I just came along?"

"Dad," I say, "how much do you know about green-screening?"

"Well, nothing. But I don't have to. I could just be the Yoda of video—you know, sitting there looking wise. You'd do everything and look over to me every so often, and I'd nod and say deep stuff. You know. *Film and life are one. The essence of both is light. Focus is a function—*"

I have to put this fire out now. What if they asked him about *Stairway to Heaven*? "I know, I know," I cut in. "I just think this would be easier. Please? It would really help."

I tell Jer roughly what I want him to say, then coach him through a couple of takes. At first, being Jer, he's too enthusiastic. "Slow down," I tell him. "Remember, you're not feeling so good."

"You're the director. How about I cough a little while I'm talking?"

Jer nails it on the next try. His shoulders slump, and his eyes half close. His voice shrinks to a scratchy whisper. He does a dry little cough just before he mutters, "Spencer knows exactly what I need. I know you can all deliver, so go for it. Then we can edit this concept into a gem we'll all be proud of. Remember, if *you* look bad, *we* look bad." He sinks back in the chair and gives a crooked little smile, as if he's worn out.

"Wow, that was great." I'm truly impressed.

Jer grins. "That was me doing Marlon Brando doing the Godfather. We were workshopping a parody version in the Parkdale Players years ago."

"Did I tell you that *you look bad, we look bad* bit?"

"Don't think so." Jer shrugs. "Just an ad lib. I mean, it stands to reason."

"Totally. I love it."

"Cool. Did you want to do it again? I'd forgotten how much I like improv. Get it from your granddad, I guess." Jer's dad was a mime artist in San Francisco back in the sixties. He even met Jerry Garcia.

"No, thanks. This is great."

"And you're sure you don't need me there tomorrow?"

"I'm on it, Dad."

Thirteen

Jer drops me off at school the next morning. He frowns as we roll past Fifteenth Street. Thoughts of Bunny, I guess.

A green-screen room is pretty much what it sounds like, a room with a screen of green fabric or paper that covers a wall and unrolls across the floor as well, to make a totally blank background. You film the actors or objects in front of the screen, and then later you can add in any background you want from other footage. It's way cheaper than location shooting or building complicated sets.

You do have to be careful about a few things though. One is keeping the background screen absolutely uniform. The room has its own set of Kino Flos, so first I do a preliminary setup of cross and back lighting that should eliminate shadows. Then, with all the lights on, I check the screen for holes, wrinkles and faded patches. It's a little rough around the edges, and the floor part is a bit dirty, but otherwise it's good.

Next, I set up the camera and mark the position with tape on the floor. I put my clipboard with the list of shots beside it. I plug in my computer and portable speakers. "Kingpin" is in a file, ready to play. Then I go hunt for the other key piece of equipment—a stepladder. It's good to always have one nearby so you can climb up to fix the screen if it starts to sag. It also comes in handy for cool shots from odd angles. This is film school, after all.

Having so much to do is good for me, because it cuts down on worry time. We don't have long. I don't think the shots are technically difficult, but getting BlueGrap to do some of them might be. On the weekend I was mostly filming them doing their thing, but now I'm literally calling the shots. Saying *you look good, we look good* isn't going to help much if they think they're looking dumb. And really, who wouldn't think they look dumb wearing badly fitting Elvis costumes? I would, believe me. Does being able to feel BlueGrap's pain make me a better director? Probably not. I look at the bag of costumes and decide not to get them out just yet. Instead I dig out my phone with Jer's video on it and put it with the shot list, as insurance. *Workingman's Dead* is playing on the computer to set the mood.

Max comes bopping in first, with day-old chocolate cake to share for breakfast. Dev and Kate arrive together five minutes later, toting instrument cases and coffees.

"Where's Andy?" I ask as Max passes me a piece of cake.

He answers with a question. "How late was he when he picked you up last Friday?"

"About an hour. Hey, how did you know he was late?"

"He runs on Andy time. An hour late is early for him. How long have we got the room?"

"Three hours."

"With luck he'll be here before we're done. Where's Jer?"

Kate and Dev laser in on my answer.

"Well, um..."

They're already frowning. I'm reaching for my phone when the door opens. In walks Jer.

Fourteen

Or maybe I should say in *totters* Jer. Or Ancient Jer. Ghost of Jer. Jer II. I don't know, but it's not the Jer who dropped me off half an hour ago, the one who said, "Break a leg" and headed to the hardware store to buy more paint stripper and scraper blades.

His shoulders are slumped, and he's dragging one foot a little. His left arm hangs at his side, and his right leans on a cane that's been in our hall closet since Deb tore her Achilles tendon playing badminton three years ago. He's also wearing an oversized shirt that belonged to her dad, my grandpa David. It hangs off Jer's neck as if he's lost fifty pounds. His face is pale behind his mirrored aviators, and his beard looks grayer too.

"Jerry!" everybody cries. They start for him. I'm too stunned to move. A phrase I sometimes hear Deb use as she marks essays pops into my head: *What fresh hell is this?*

Jer stops just inside the door, panting a little, as if getting in here has pretty much done him in for the day. A crooked smile flickers.

"You made it," gushes Kate.

Jer nods a head that weighs a hundred pounds. "And I wish I could stay. Spencer's probably told you I'm a little under the weather." Jer's voice is that scratchy whisper he used on the phone video.

"Yeah, man. Sorry to hear that," Max says. "Do you want a piece of cake?"

"Can't. Doctor's orders. I'm not even supposed to be here. I needed things from the office, and I had to tell you guys something." He pauses to pant some more.

"What is it, Jer?" Dev leans in. "You want a chair or something?"

"No, no. Like I said, can't stay."

That's a relief. On the other hand, he hasn't left yet.

"I just wanted to say that, first of all, you are the most promising new talent I've come across in a long time. This whole thing is about helping us help you go all the way. That's why I've entrusted this shoot to Spencer. He's my guy. He knows exactly what we need from you today. It could be challenging, but I know you can do it. It's a great concept—you'll love it when you see."

"What *is* the concept, Jer?" Kate asks. "I mean, we're totally with you, but we'd love to know."

Jer breaks into a cyclone of coughing. Hands reach to steady him.

"Sorry. Gotta see it to understand it. Trust us if it seems weird now," he gasps. "We'll talk later. Don't worry, under control. Just follow Spencer."

He shuffles out the door.

"Stay strong for *Stairway*," Max calls. Jer twitches, then keeps on going, closing the door behind him. I start to breathe again.

Dev turns to me. "What do we need to do?"

He's with me. I can feel them all with me. I owe Jer a solid, big-time. I reach for the bag of costumes.

Fifteen

"We have to *what?*"

Forget owing Jer. They're not with me anymore. I should have done the easy shots with them first. "Just jump down from the ladder and run out of the shot. Then we'll get another shot walking."

"Wearing that." Kate jabs an accusing finger at a costume drooping from its hanger. It's a white jumpsuit with a low neck, high collar and a massive belt at the waist. Rhinestones are spattered across it like bad acne.

"Well, yeah," I say. "Whichever one fits best. It's simple."

"But what for?" Max bobs in disbelief. Cake crumbs frost his lumberjack beard, kind of like the rhinestones.

"Well, I don't know exactly." I wish this wasn't so close to the truth. "But that's what Jer wants." Despite the air conditioning, I feel a trickle of sweat. Things are slipping away from me, and we haven't even started yet. If the Jer card won't do it, what the heck will?

"The track has nothing to do with Elvis!" Crumbs dance onto the green-screen floor. I ease Max away from it. "Hey, man," I say, "All I know is this. Remember Andy said the songs are all about moving?"

"They're not songs, they're *raps*. They're poetry! And they're not Andy's, they're mine."

"Sorry. My bad. Anyway, I told Jer what Andy said, and Jer told me that Elvis was a Cadillac guy, so he moves, right? And he was called the King."

"But 'Kingpin' isn't about Elvis! That's not what I was writing about. Elvis isn't from Compton!"

"Neither are you," Dev points out. *Thank you, Dev.* He holds up another jumpsuit on its hanger. His may be the only one that fits properly. I wonder how it will look with his glasses.

"I know," I say to Max. "But Elvis is a strong visual. Instant recognition. The pictures aren't supposed to, um, replay the lyrics. It's, like, a parallel story."

Max is winding up for another point, but I cut him off with something I just thought of. "'Kingpin' is your rap, right? It spoke to Jer. It was his favorite one, right? People are going to get what they want out of your stuff, even if it isn't exactly what you meant to begin with." Deb has a whole long speech about this and a fancy name for it, but I can't remember it right now. "You can't control it, Max. I mean, *Stairway to Heaven* won't show an actual stairway to heaven, right?"

"What will it show?" That's Dev again. He's still eyeing the jumpsuit. I take back my thank-you and say, "An escalator at a shopping mall." Don't ask me why.

"That's actually pretty cool." Dev nods.

I ignore him and plunge on. "That's why Jer is so good. It's unexpected. It's a vision thing. He flashed on Elvis. And that's all it will be, just quick flashes. A few only."

"Uh-huh," Kate cuts in. "But for a few 'quick flashes' we look like idiots. This is supposed to be a serious band, a new musical hybrid."

I spin to her. "But you are! You won't look like idiots. You'll look as if you have a sense of humor." Which I am totally beginning to believe Kate does not have.

"Hey, Kay," Dev says, "it may not even matter." He hoists an eyebrow. *Thank you again, Dev.* I turn back to Max. He scratches his beard. More crumbs fall.

"I dunno, man. Kate's right. It's serious work. Like a cross-pollination, you know? A hybrid genre. I don't want to dumb it down."

This is sounding like eleventh-grade biology, which I almost failed. "It's not dumbing down," I say, "it's balancing. Hey, remember that great close-up of you thinking over the vocal takes? How serious can you get? That whole shot is just screaming *think*, right? *Serious.* But then we show your playful side. You're entertaining when you perform, right? Same thing."

Boy, I hope it is, because I'm running out of things to say. This Elvis shtick is all I have to add to my idea, and if I can't get them to do it, I too will be down the rabbit hole—which is close to my idea but not as much fun.

"Okay." Max finally nods. "Let's try it. But in the end, if it doesn't work it comes out, right?"

"You'll know by Friday," I tell him, which is also the day I can cash those checks. "*You guys.*" I sigh. "Jer said you're the most promising talent he's ever seen. Trust him. He's not going to make you look bad. You look bad, we look bad, remember? Now c'mon. We have to use this time."

I look at Kate. She looks at Dev and then me. "This health thing hasn't affected Jer's brain, right?" she says.

"Kaaaate." I go for Deb's voice when she's especially bummed with Bunny or me.

She looks at Dev, then back at me, again. Then she nods too. If film school doesn't work out, I just might have a future selling used cars.

Sixteen

I give everyone a chance to settle down, and Andy time to get here, by walking them through how things will work. Andy doesn't arrive, so we start without him. I warm everybody up by having them play and lip-synch along to "Kingpin" in front of the screen. I shoot a master, and then we do it again for some close-ups.

Then, still without Andy, it's Elvis time. Max and Dev put on the jumpsuits first. Kate digs into the bag of safety pins Deb sent along and does her best to make the costumes fit better. I check lighting and camera. "Okay, just for fun first. Jump up and down." Max bounces like a ping-pong ball on Red Bull. Dev looks like he doesn't want to mess his hair. I back up the camera and try something else. "Okay, great,"

I lie. Then I improvise. "Um, one at a time, just run a step or two and then jump across the screen."

They start to get into it a little more. Next I ask them to strut past the camera in profile. Not so good. Max sways like a rubberized race walker. Dev is stiffer than a wooden soldier. "Even better!" I lie again. I put the camera back in its original spot, aimed dead center at the green screen. Max climbs the ladder, and we do a couple of test jumps. Naturally, it's trickier than I thought it would be. Max has to jump down from the ladder into the shot, look both ways and then run out to his right. It takes a few tries to get it.

And Max had it easy—he's not carrying an instrument. Max and Kate head out to the washrooms to trade off the small costume, and Dev, guitar in hand, climbs the ladder. Slowly. He clutches the top. "I don't like heights," he confesses.

"That's cool. Jump down now then. Camera's running."

"I don't want to let go of the ladder."

"Well, if you're scared of heights, just jump down," I tell him. What's the big deal?

"*I don't want to let go of the ladder.*"

I'm beginning to see what Deb means about fresh hells. Before I can figure out how to convince him to jump, the door bangs open. Dev cries out, the ladder wobbles, and Dev drops like a rock, right into the center of the shot. The ladder crashes down. Someone shouts. Dev stumbles. "Run out, run out!" I yell. Dev runs.

Unfortunately, he picks the wrong way, and his guitar spears Andy, who has walked in, banjo case in one hand and the world's largest takeout coffee in the other. Andy blats out an "Ooof!" and a creamy brown arc sails across the room, splattering the green screen and my camera. "Am I late?" Andy gasps, rubbing his stomach. Today's hat, a gray topper, has hit the floor.

Let's just say things go up and down from there. Most of the coffee has landed on my equipment and on the floor part of the screen. I clean up the camera as best I can with my T-shirt and one that turns out to be Dev's. Everything still seems to work, and I manage to avoid enough of the splotches on the screen to frame a really tight shot of Kate jumping, holding her viola. On the downside, my gear now smells like coffee, and the stains on the screen mean I can't get the running and walking shots I'd planned. And Andy can't even squeeze into the costume, which, although it makes him look more like the real Elvis, means I can't film him at all.

BlueGrap does not seem heartbroken about any of this. "So, are we done?" Kate asks, tossing her jumpsuit back to me.

"I'll have to talk to Jer," I say, even though I know we're not done. I've got a hole in my idea a mile wide, and no clue how to fill it. "There are a whole bunch of shots we didn't get. We might have to shoot again tomorrow afternoon, as soon as I finish work. Can everyone make that?"

"Sure, but I gotta get to work *now,*" Max calls, hustling out the door. "Leavin' the rest of the cake for y'all. Text me place and time."

"Text us too." Dev and Kate follow. As they go out the door I hear Kate say, "How pointless is this?"

Andy tilts back his top hat as he watches them leave. "Hey, really sorry about that, man. Will you have to pay for the screen or anything?"

There are dark blotches where I've soaked it to get the coffee out. "It should be okay when it dries. I've been in here when it's happened before. I think they clean them every so often."

"No kidding? That's good then. Sorry I was late. Things came up."

For a second I think about calling Andy out on that, but then let it go. For one thing, he's stuck around to help me pack up. And he's the only one who seems to take me seriously. For another, I've got way bigger things to worry about. I didn't get all the shots I need, I don't know what to replace them with, and I'm running out of time—big-time.

"You need a ride?" Andy asks as we finish.

"Thanks, Andy. That would be great. I've got to get these costumes back."

I sign out with the secretary in the department office and return the room key. I tell her about the screen, and that it just needs some drying time. She frowns and writes down my student number, twice. She also tells me that no, there are no rooms available tomorrow.

I add maybe damaging the screen and having to pay for it to my load of worries. Andy drives me to the costume shop in the hearse. I stare down Fifteenth Street as we pass, at the graffiti-covered wall of the gym where the Posse hangs out. In a movie, there would be something scrawled in the graffiti that gives me a genius-type idea. In real life, the graffiti doesn't tell me a thing except that the Fifteenth Street Posse are bad spellers. I have a sudden urge to tell Andy that this is Scratch's real address, but I don't. That's not going to help with anything. He lets me out in front of the shop. "Text me what we're doin' tomorrow," he calls as he drives off. I wish I knew.

Seventeen

I trudge up the porch steps at O'Toole Central as Jer comes out the front door, dressed for jogging. He looks a lot healthier than the last time I saw him.

"How'd I do?" he says. "Did it help? Sorry I didn't warn you, but I thought it would play more naturally if we just winged it. I liked the way you hung back."

"Thanks," I say. "It was a surprise, but it was good. They went for it."

"You're looking a little bedraggled there. Did something happen?"

"Oh, just a bunch of other stuff went wrong. I didn't get all the shots I needed. I'll figure something out."

Jer is bouncing on his toes now, getting ready for his run. "Well, if there's anything I can do to help, just tell me." I start inside. "Hey," he calls after me, "how did they know about the stairs?"

"Just a lucky guess."

"Huh. Well, don't breathe too much in there. That paint stripper was giving me a headache. I need some fresh air."

Jer trots off. There's a nasty chemical tang inside the house. At least it overpowers the coffee smell of my T-shirt. The stairway doesn't seem much different. I go up to change. Then I head into the kitchen, pour a glass of juice, heat up some mac and cheese and plunk myself down with my laptop. I dump today's footage from the Canon's memory card into the computer. Not a lot to show for a whole morning's work. A lip-synched performance, some useless bouncing and jumping and a quick shot of an empty green screen disappearing behind a muddy splash of coffee.

To say this is depressing is an understatement. Even sadder are all the shots I didn't get. No Andy. And I didn't get the good running and walking shots I needed to edit into the city background. There's going to be too much recording session and not enough action to tell any kind of story. Kate is right—BlueGrap is going to look like a bunch of idiots. *You look bad, we look bad.*

I sit at the kitchen table, my brain congealing like the mac and cheese. AmberLea is still out of cell range, Bunny is out of the picture, and I think Jer has done all he can do. I'm on my own. How can *I* rescue this?

All I know is that I can't sit here any longer. At the very least I can film a location for their green-screen performance, even if that performance is Andy-free. Filming something—anything—might give me another idea. I know exactly where to go.

I pack my camera, tripod and laptop and bike it back to Fifteenth Street. I have to make this quick. My shift starts at five.

When I get there, the setting is perfect. The sun is still quite high, so the graffiti-covered wall of the gym glows, with just a touch of shadow down near the base. Nobody is parked in front of it. A guy leans against one end of the wall, texting. Above his head I see a tag in yellow paint: *FREE BUNY.*

I'll make sure to get that in a shot somehow. Another guy is wandering up the alley with a gym bag, but otherwise the sidewalk is clear. I set up fast and turn on my laptop to double-check distance and angle on this morning's shots. I'll need to be in the street, a few feet out from the gym-side curb. I figure I'll also need a master shot of the whole wall for backup. I'm peering through the viewfinder when behind me a voice asks softly, "Looking for something?"

I jump up so fast I almost knock over the tripod. Scratch stands there watching me from behind his Ray-Bans. Today he's all in black, not even the silk scarf showing.

"Hey," I say lamely.

"What are you doing?"

"Shooting some exteriors. We were green-screening this morning and—"

Scratch cuts me off with a hiss. "Get that camera outta here. Now."

"But it's the perfect location."

"You're not listening, Buffalo Boy. Five seconds or T-Bird packs it for you. He's good at compacting."

I glance down the sidewalk. The guy leaning against the wall is moving our way. I start packing up. Fast. "But what the..." I sputter. "I need the shot. I thought you'd like it, a little in-joke, you know. And I'm running out of time and—"

"I got meetings this afternoon. With very private people. They like to keep it that way. It's a good thing T-Bird recognized you. If one of them had come along and seen you filming, they'd have probably fed both of us your camera. I shouldn't even be near you right now. The whole neighborhood probably thinks you're a cop."

"*Me?*" I'm five foot eight, eighteen years old, and I weigh maybe one forty-five including my glasses.

"I thought you were sharper than this, Buffalo Boy."

By now I've got everything stowed and slung and I'm straddling my bike. I know Scratch is a bad dude, but I've had a worse day. Plus he pulled a fast one with my advance check. I can't hold back.

"Well, excuuuuuse me," I say. "I thought you were a music mogul now and you wanted this done fast."

Scratch glances at his watch, then softens a little. "Look, you want to film here, you ask permission, just like anyplace else."

"Okay, can I film here tomorrow afternoon? I gotta get this done."

He nods. "What time?"

"Two thirty. Won't take long."

"How long?"

"Maybe an hour."

"All right. Anything else you need?"

"Nothing parked on the street in front."

He nods again. "I won't be here. Posse will know. You won't be hassled. And BlueGrap doesn't know I got anything to do with this place. Clear?"

"Clear."

"They cooperating?"

"We're good."

Scratch starts to turn away. He looks back at me. "You ever heard of a music guy name of Alex Pulodnikov? Little Puddles?"

I shake my head. "What is he, a Russian rapper?"

"Something like. Just wondering. How about Fingers Donovan?"

"Did he play guitar in Black Sabbath?"

Scratch blows out something between a snort and a sigh. "Ask Jerry if he knows. He's got contacts in the biz." He turns away, then looks back. "The dude still sick?"

"A little better. But don't worry—he's still all over this."

He's gone before I can mention the check. That's okay. I think I just got my idea instead.

Eighteen

It's a gamble, but it's all I've got. Everyone is expecting to shoot tomorrow. If we can't use the green screen, we'll do it the old-fashioned way. On location. Weather permitting, shooting will be the easy part. The tough part will be convincing BlueGrap to be silly in public instead of in a studio.

As I make complicated coffees for people all evening, I try to picture Kate (especially Kate) cheerfully agreeing to run around Fifteenth Street in an Elvis suit. It's not a vision that comes easily. Then there's the little matter of stuffing Andy into one of the costumes. Ain't gonna happen, as Jer likes to say. I'm doing my last double low-fat mochaccino soy chai latte when I flash on the possible answer to both problems. It'll be tricky to pull off, and a long shot, given today's happenings, but it's not going to kill me. I wish I could say the same for Jer.

When I get home Deb and Jer are playing crib at the kitchen table. I ask if either of them could stop by the costume shop the next morning and get the Elvis suits again. Deb has a department meeting at the university, but Jer is up for it. "If you just bring them here I'll grab them on my way to the shoot," I say as Deb slaps down cards and moves her pin up the board. She's a take-no-prisoners player.

Jer nods as he gathers up the deck and squares it to shuffle. "Where are you shooting?"

If there is one place in the world I can't tell my parents we're shooting at, it's the headquarters of the Fifteenth Street Posse. And you know my parental policy: keep things as general as possible. "Oh, a couple of places. Just wrap-up stuff. Depends how it goes. We may have to shoot some at their rehearsal space." There is a possibility of this, so it's my concrete contribution. It's also enough to give me a heart-attack thought. "But don't come by," I add really fast. "Today was plenty. We don't want to overdo it."

Deb gives me a look. "I hear your dad finally got to do his Godfather impersonation this morning. He was so disappointed when the Parkdale Players didn't do that show."

"Well, he was great," I say. "It was worth waiting for."

"Thank you," says Jer, shuffling cards. "Took a while to get the flour out of my beard."

Now she gives us both a look. "You know, despite the Machiavelli talk, telling the truth might have been just as effective. Just saying."

Jer deals. "You may be right. Anyway, never fear, Spence. I won't be there for a reprise, Scout's honor. I'd imagine you need to get this done and get editing ASAP."

He is so right. With everything under control—I even have an almost-complete storyline for the video—I head to my room to watch *The Stunt Man* again for inspiration and then flake out early. I'm going to have to be on my game first thing in the morning.

And the next morning is the only time I've ever been glad to be doing a clopen. Otherwise I would have had to get up specially at 4:45 AM to send the text I've written to get things rolling:

Jer died last night. Left last instructions for a location shoot 1:30 this aft, 15th St & Lakeshore. Same clothes as cottage. He was thinking about you until the end. Let's do this for him.

Say what you want (don't tell Deb), but right now the results are what count. I can explain it all to BlueGrap later, at the MTV video awards or the Grammys or someplace. Or even as soon as they see how cool it all is and I cash the checks. I send the text to Max, Dev and Kate. I send a slightly different one to Andy. On his, I set the shoot for noon and ask him to dress in black and wear his Greek fisherman's cap and Holstein shoes. Budgeting for Andy Time, that ought to bring him in right on schedule.

Biking to work, I review my plan for the day. I'm working until eleven. Jer will pick up the Elvis suits this morning and put them with my gear, which is packed and ready in the front hall at O'Toole Central. I'll ride home, change and head straight to Fifteenth Street to set up. Then, when the band arrives, it will be persuading time. I'm hoping the bad news about Jer will leave them soft as play dough. As insurance I've still got Jer's video on my cell phone. If I need a "last message" from the big guy to tip the balance, I'll play it. "Shameless" has become my middle name.

The location shots themselves should be fairly simple. The weather forecast is for sunshine. We don't need sound. We'll be able to park the hearse right in front of the gym's graffiti-covered wall. Scratch's posse should keep us from being disturbed. If we can get them done quickly, I'll ask everybody to go back to the rehearsal space for a quick "interview" segment I probably won't use but which will make them feel they are being taken seriously. We can be done by supper. I can start editing tonight, and I don't have to be back at work until Sunday.

Simple. Straightforward. So why am I so nervous? I'll tell you why. Persuading time. The whole project depends on whether I can pull it off.

When the morning-commuter coffee rush is over I step outside to take my break in non-caffeinated air. I check my phone and find texts from Dev and Max saying they're sorry to hear the news and that they'll be there. I'm looking for one from Kate (I can't imagine Andy being up yet) when someone calls my name. I look up and there she is, hurrying along the sidewalk toward me. "Spencer," she says again, coming up close. "Oh, Spencer, I'm so sorry," and then she's giving me a hug, saying close to my ear, "And we just saw him yesterday."

I'm so surprised I don't know what to do. I give her a kind-of hug back.

"You were close, weren't you? You had to be when he trusted you so much." She holds my shoulders at arm's length. "Listen, be strong. We can totally get through this. We'll help."

"R-right." I nod. Wow, have I ever misjudged Kate.

"Were you there when he...?"

"Ah, no, I just...they..."

"Just his family? Did he have much family?"

"Well, the usual, I guess."

"Do you know about a funeral?"

"Um, no, but I think it will just be, you know... family. Or maybe nothing—he's already been cremated." Why am I babbling like an idiot? I'll tell you why. Because over Kate's shoulder, guess who I've just spotted, cheerfully bustling our way with my gear and a bag from the costume shop?

You're right. It's Jer. I don't know what my face does, but Kate's forehead creases in confusion. She turns.

The whole thing unfolds in something like slow motion. Jer's eyes widen, and somehow in midstride he slows down, and his shoulders sag. His last couple of steps become a shuffle. It's a valiant effort if I ever saw one. Or maybe a Valium effort. "Well," he whispers. "Kate, right? I didn't—"

"You're dead." Kate cuts him off in a voice as ghostly as Jer should be.

Jer does a little chuckle-cough. "Well, the rumors of my death have been greatly exaggerated, as they say."

This does not help. Kate swivels between us, lasering a look that would reduce a medium-sized planet to a mound of smoking cinders. In a movie, I'd have a line of comic patter that would smooth this all over. Or maybe I'd be quick-witted enough to pretend I was astonished too.

This is not a movie. There's a silence that stretches out way past painful, then, "What's going on?" Kate's voice has sharpened. "What is this, some kind of trick? Some kind of sick...stunt?" Her voice gets quieter instead of louder, which makes it even scarier. She turns to Jer. "He said—" She turns to me. "What are you trying to do? Are you trying to steal this? Jer's the one we're supposed to be working with, not some student gofer." She swings back to Jer. "You should get rid of him. He's a sicko. He's taking advantage of you. Or are you dumping him on us while you work with Led Zeppelin? We're not good enough for you? You're both sickos. Manipulative sickos. I *hate* Led Zeppelin." Her phone is out, and she's texting furiously. "Wait'll Scratch hears about this. Screw filming, I'm calling a meeting at the studio. You better be there. And you better explain."

"I'm working until eleven," is all I can come up with.

"At 11:01 then. I don't know what this is about, but you're the one that's dead." She stalks away, still stabbing at her phone screen.

Jer watches her go, then looks at me. He smiles bleakly. "Sorry, Spence. Not quite sure what happened there."

"No worries," I sigh. "Just another idea gone wrong." I can feel my shoulders sagging.

Jer hefts the gear and costume bag. "I just wanted to bring you these, save you making a trip home. I know their rehearsal space is in the other direction."

"Yeah. No. Thanks. It is." There's no point mentioning Fifteenth Street.

"What did she mean, I'm dead?"

"Could I explain later?"

"Sure. And I'm working with Led Zeppelin?"

"Could I explain that later too?"

Jer nods. "On the lighter side, if there is one, look what else I got at the costume shop." Jer's wearing his old tweed sport coat over his T-shirt. He pokes a lapel at me. On it a little plastic Elvis bust is sneering his jump-suited heart out.

"Should I take this stuff home?" Jer asks, "or do you want me to come with you and explain?"

"No thanks," I say. All at once I'm standing up straight. "I'll handle it, and I'll take the stuff. But there is something else you could do for me."

I fire off another text to Andy.

Nineteen

After work I load up my gear and bike down to the Rehearsal Factory. I'm nervous, but not as nervous as I was about my original plan. Now I really know what I have to do.

I climb the stairs to find Max, Dev and Kate waiting for me. I wouldn't say they look like gangstas, but they're not happy hobbits either. They have a right to be upset. They start in on me as soon as I walk in.

"All right," snarls Max. "What's going on?"

"Nothing just yet." I'm aiming for chipper, but I think maybe I only manage chipped.

"Where's Jer?" Dev cuts in. "Kate saw him. What's with this 'he's dead' stuff?"

Max jumps back in. "*What's going on?*"

I push up my glasses, straighten to my full not-very-tallness and take a deep, semishaky breath. "Let's get something straight, okay? Scratch hired *me* to do your video. Not Jer. I asked Jer along so I wouldn't get carded at the Emmett. When you liked him, it made it easier for me to work."

"Of course we liked him," snaps Kate. "He's a film prof—he works with the pros. We wanted this to be *great*, not a term project for a...what are you, *first year*?"

"So what are you, Beethoven?" That just pops out. They all jerk back a little. "Anyway, Jer's not a film prof."

"Okay, a filmmaker."

"He's not that either."

"Well, what is he?"

"He's my dad."

"Your *dad*?" That's all three at once, in the best harmony they've ever had. Then it breaks down.

"What the—?"

"Holy—"

"I can't believe this!"

"So this was all a waste," Kate says. "A joke. All that time, all that—"

"Money?" I say. "It's not your money. It's Scratch's. Besides, I'm not getting paid a million bucks, and I haven't even cashed a check yet for anything."

"Because there's probably no video, is there?" Dev shakes his head.

"Oh, there will be. If you want there to be. I only need three more shots before I edit. I'll get them as soon as Andy shows up."

Max snorts in disbelief.

"Listen," I say, "I tricked you. I admit it. I didn't like doing it, but Scratch wanted results. Do *you* want results?" Silence. "Do you trust Scratch?" They nod. It's a bad answer, when you think about it, but I don't say that.

"He's worked with all kinds of people," says Dev. *He sure has*, I think, *just not the kind you're thinking of.* "All right then," I say. "And do I have to remind you *who he chose* to work with on your video?" They look at me. It occurs to me that I may be channeling Deb here. It also occurs to me that maybe I should have had this conversation with BlueGrap at the start.

Don't you hate it when your mom's advice turns out to be right?

I finish up with, "So if you think you know better than Scratch, just tell him, and I'll walk. I don't owe anybody anything."

"We've been trying to reach him," Max says. "He's not returning our texts."

"He's probably in a meeting," Kate says.

"Fine," I say. "Would you rather I tell him that *you* walked?"

A pause.

"You get these shots," Dev asks, "how long until you're done?"

"I'll have a rough cut in twenty-four hours, right on time," I say with a confidence I don't feel. "Just another all-nighter at the screen. I'll show you six o'clock tomorrow, right here."

No one leaves. Phones come out as we settle in to wait for Andy. "Any of you ever heard of a rapper named Little Puddles? A guitar player named Fingers Donovan?" I ask, trying to lighten the mood. They look at me as if I'm crazy. I get out my camera.

The next half hour is frosty for May. Andy finally arrives shortly past noon, incredibly early for him. He's dressed the way I asked him to be and all cheery. "Hey, everybody. What's rockin'? What's this about Jer? What do I have to do?"

I reach in my pocket and pull out Jer's new pin. "You and I have to go for a drive."

Twenty

I was wrong about the twenty-four hours. It only takes twenty-three and a half, after Andy and I finish, and that's including the time I was asleep at the computer (I'm not sure for how long). There are a couple of wonky bits, some wobbly cuts and transitions. Also, I hadn't noticed that Max was wearing green socks. The editing program blots out anything green, so there are a couple of places where, if you watch closely, it looks like his feet aren't attached to his body. On the whole, though, it's a good rough cut. I haven't even had to use any cow footage. I text Scratch and BlueGrap to remind them about our six o'clock meeting, then set the alarm on my phone and crash for a couple of hours.

It takes Deb plus the alarm to wake me at four thirty. I grab a shower and head downstairs for a snack. Jer has clearly been working on the stairway. He's making real progress. He turns from the kitchen counter as I come in. "Done?" I nod as he passes me a big glass of juice and an extra-thick peanut butter sandwich. "Got time to show it to me?"

I pause in midswallow. But hey, Jer did help with this, and now I'm a pro. When BlueGrap posts the final edit, the world will see. "Sure," I say. I put down my juice and go get my computer.

I'm not sure why showing something to my dad makes me more nervous than the thought of showing it to a grumpy band that thinks I've manipulated them into looking like idiots, but it does. Jer pours himself a coffee and adds milk. I try to ignore the smell as we settle at the kitchen table. "Oops, sorry," says Jer, noticing.

"No worries." I press *Play.*

The screen goes black, and there's ambient noise my camera microphone caught as BlueGrap prepped that first night at Rehearsal Factory: voices, a viola flourish, a guitar chord, the rattle of a tambourine. Then the rhythm and bass loops for "Kingpin" jump in, and the screen comes alive to the hearse barreling at the camera down that country road, dust boiling behind it. As the instruments continue, we cut to a shot of the whole band playing, then to a close-up of Max as he starts to rap. Back to the hearse, pulling up to a curb. The driver's door with the Parade Marshal sign opens, and out step the Holstein shoes. Cut to a shot of my cell-phone screen as Jer's dying-Godfather pep talk plays silently below the music, then close-ups of the band huddled and nodding in concentration as they seem to watch it (really, they were listening to a playback at the cottage). Next are tight shots of packing up I got from the first night's rehearsal—instrument cases snapping shut, that kind of thing—and then they're in the pontoon boat, heading across the river.

As "Kingpin" continues we cut to a bumper-level shot of the hearse stopping, edited too tight to show it's the hearse. This time the passenger door opens and out come feet—Dev's, Kate's, Max's bare feet with a fringe of towel showing above them, and Andy's, but now he has sneakers on, instead of the Holsteins. They march down the street. Max in the towel makes a nicely weird touch I think he'll like. Cut to a segment of BlueGrap playing, a montage of Kate bowing and Dev and Andy picking, then cutting to faces as they get to the second chorus for the call and response. My favorite bit is coming up. As Max raps "*down the rabbit hole*" there's a quick cut to him disappearing off the cottage deck, which, thanks to green-screening and careful editing into some of the footage I shot yesterday afternoon, ends with him dropping down in front of the gym wall on Fifteenth Street, wearing an Elvis suit, and darting out of the frame. He's followed instantly by Kate and Dev in their Elvis suits.

They swing into the final verse in another montage, but they're performing in front of the gym wall. Cut to Holstein shoes at the bottom of crossed black-jeaned legs, shot from the sidewalk. Pan up to show it's Andy, fisherman's cap on, all in black except for a white dot on his lapel, leaning against the front of the hearse as if he's waiting, and in the background, across the street, the Bates and Dodds funeral parlor across from the Rehearsal Factory. This is another shot from yesterday. As they swing into the final chorus, cut to Dev in his Elvis suit, jumping. He sails across the gym wall, shrinking as he goes. Cut to Andy, still leaning against the hearse, this time shot from street side, with the gym wall as background. He rocks back as if something hits him, and there's a cheesy little gleam of light off that white dot, like the ones that show sparkling teeth in toothpaste commercials. Cut to Kate and then Max jumping, minimizing and disappearing into that white dot on Andy's chest as he rocks back twice more. The shot zooms in tight on Andy until the white dot mushrooms full screen into Jer's new Elvis head—the King pin. The zoom continues past focus until the King pin blurs into a swirl of black and white that resolves into dust boiling behind the hearse as it rumbles away down the country road. Cut to black as the song ends.

I hit *Stop*. Jer sits back and puffs out a breath. "Spence, that is *cool*."

"I love it," Deb says from behind me. I didn't know she'd come in. "It's not my music, and I don't quite get it, but I still love it."

I know it's my parents talking. I know I like to make jokes about their taste. I know that, to tell you the truth, I don't quite get the story I'm telling in the video either. But it *feels* like a story, and when Deb and Jer say they like it, I feel as if I just got invited to Hollywood. "It's just a rough cut," is all I can come up with. I'm pretty sure I'm blushing. "I want to work in the shoes somehow at the beginning."

Immediately Jer is on the case. "Hey, what if you came out of that first black screen to them?"

"Like, before the hearse?"

"Yeah! And then at the end—"

We talk it over. No one seems to have noticed Max's disconnected feet or the *FREE BUNY* tag high up on the brick wall.

Deb interrupts. "If Spence is meeting the band at six, he'd better get moving."

"Right!" Jer jumps up.

"Hey, Dad?" I say. "Thanks."

Twenty-One

I get to the Rehearsal Factory on time. I slip past smokers and gig bags and head upstairs. Will BlueGrap like the video? Will Scratch like the video? I wish I'd had time to cash the checks first. But hey, this way it will be like a point of honor that I haven't—and you better believe I'll hit the bank before I do any more editing.

When I get to BlueGrap's studio, the door is closed. Electric-guitar licks sound faintly behind it. I knock, then open the door. Guitar blasts me. Andy sits facing an amp, picking. He's wearing the Holstein shoes and a slouchy tweed newsboy cap. Earbuds run to his phone on top of the amp. He breaks off when he sees me, clicking off his phone and popping out an earbud. He looks surprised.

"Wow," I say. "You're, uh, on time."

He laughs. "Oh, I've been here all afternoon. Lotta practicing to do. I didn't think *you'd* be coming."

"Didn't think I'd get done on time?" Now I laugh, unslinging my backpack. "Where is everybody?"

Andy squints at me. "Um, I don't think they're coming, Spencer. Didn't you get the messages? There's been kind of a good news, bad news thing."

"Messages?" I dig out my phone. It's off. I remember shutting it down for uninterrupted editing. I power it up to find a screen full of text notifications, from Scratch, Max, Dev, Kate and Andy. "Wow," I say. "Where do I start?"

"Scratch's maybe?"

I call it up.

All

Pleasure working w/you but have to split. music biz harshest hustle on the planet too many puddles and fingers. seen safer street crime. New projects mean new number so don't bother to call. Experience our paycheck. Props to Bun

happy life

"What the—he dumped you?"

Andy nods. "Looks like. Do you know what the Bun thing means? Or the puddles and fingers?"

"Yeah. Some other time. They're not important right now." Now I get Puddles and Fingers. Knowing Scratch, I should have known they weren't musicians. I say to Andy, "You know, this may not be such a bad thing. I'm not sure how much Scratch knows about the music business. And now BlueGrap has a video."

Andy nods. "Yeah, well, uh, actually the band broke up too, Spencer. That's what the other texts are about."

I hurry through the first couple. Max is joining a poetry slam collective. Dev says he and Kate have started a world-music fusion band. "We weren't getting along so well anyway." Andy sighs. "You probably caught that. Maybe it's best. Kinda bummed about Kate though. I knew she was with Dev from the cottage on. Still..." He shrugs and laughs.

"So that leaves you," I say. "Thanks to Scratch and the others, you don't have a band or Kate." And I have a video no one needs. Though I will soon also have a thousand dollars. Maybe I shouldn't complain.

Andy squints again, and his face turns a little red. “The band breakup was my fault, really. I told them I’ve been asked to tour with the Dobermans.”

“Wow, Andy.” The Dobermans won a big music talent contest last year. It was all over the Internet.

Andy scratches his almost-beard and grins. “Yeah, got a friend who roadies for them. One of their guitar players bailed right before a tour, so he told ’em to call me. I figured BlueGrap could just get a sub for me, but that’s when the texts started flying, and they all said they wanted to quit. Then Scratch messaged us in the middle of it all. Anyway, I leave in two days. I’ve got a whack of tunes to learn before I go. That’s why I’m here workin’. No rest for the wicked and that.” He laughs and rips out a stream of notes. “So did you get the video done?”

I nod. “Not that anyone is going to want to see it.”

“I wanna see it! I was just gonna take a break anyway. Let’s give ’er.” He laughs again. I pull up a chair, and we huddle over my laptop.

As the last note sounds and the screen goes black, Andy looks up, smiling. "How cool is that? That rocks, man. Good for you. I love how you wove all those bits together."

"Thanks, Andy. I guess I should send it to everybody. Do you think they'll let me post it anyway?"

"Hope so. Hey, I'll post it. Send it to me for sure. Pleasure workin' with you, man. Let's do it again. If I click with the Dobes and they need any video work done, I'll tell them who to call." Andy stands, still holding his guitar, and gives me a one-arm bro hug.

"For sure," I say, packing up. "That would be fantastic. In the meantime"—I slap the pocket with my wallet in it—"I think I'll go 'experience my paycheck.' I'm glad he already wrote me one."

Andy squints at me again. "Uh, I think he means the experience *was* our pay, Spencer." I get a feeling kind of like Max falling into the water. I should have known. Andy goes on. "The only thing he paid for was this rehearsal space."

We look at each other. "Maybe I'd better move my stuff out now," Andy says, flicking off his amp.

I help him carry his gear downstairs. The hearse is parked around back. We load in the guitar, amps and pedals. Looking at the hearse again, I ask, "Hey, Andy, do you think I could film the hearse again sometime this summer?"

"Absolutely, man. Why?"

"I'm getting this idea for a short film," I say slowly. "The hearse might come in really handy."

"Just say the word. Text or email. If I'm not around, it'll be at my folks' place. And hey, if you need music for it, I'd be happy."

"Wow. Cool. Will do. Think zombie Elvis imitators."

He laughs. "Doesn't everybody?"

"I hope not." I wave as he pulls away, then walk back to my bike. All things considered, I feel pretty good. If I can't cash them, I at least have my first souvenir worthless professional paychecks, suitable for framing or bulletin board. And I have a video I can probably use for some kind of assignment next year, and a possible in with an up-and-coming band for video work. Not to mention I know where to get a hearse and a music score for what could turn out to be a great new project. Wait until I run the zombie idea past

AmberLea. I bet Bun will like it too. Maybe he can help when he gets out. And you know, maybe I'll talk it over with Jer too. It could give me a whole new point of view.

Acknowledgments

One of the best parts of writing is meeting interesting folks who spark the stories. Many people were generous with their time and talents as I wrote this, and I owe them all big-time.

First, my thanks to everyone in Union Duke and to Ian McKeown and Jim Bowskill for sharing their music, good humor, experiences and the hearse. It's always a joy to hear them and play with them.

Also, my thanks to Rob Quartly, who provided me with much-needed tech expertise about film and video. Anything right in what Spencer does is thanks to Rob. Anything wrong is entirely my fault.

Thanks also to my writing buddy Richard Scrimger, who kindly loaned me his character Scratch for the second time. Scratch originally appears in Richard's Seven (the series) novel *Ink Me*.

This would not be a book without the help of David Bennett at the Transatlantic Agency and all the wonderful people at Orca Books. My especial thanks to Tanya Trafford for her deft editing.

Last but not least, as always my thanks to Margaret, who never complains no matter how many times I practice a song, even when I get it wrong every time.

TED STAUNTON is the award-winning author of many books for young people, including three others starring Spencer O'Toole—*Speed, Coda* and *Jump Cut* from the various Seven series. When not creating stories, Ted writes music and plays in the Maple Leaf Champions Jug Band. For more information, visit www.tedstauntonbooks.com.

AN EXCERPT FROM

POP QUIZ
BY TOM RYAN

978-1-4598-1222-2 PB
978-1-4598-1223-9 PDF . 978-1-4598-1224-6 EPUB

AIDEN DIDN'T MEAN TO EAVESDROP...

I walk up the front steps and push through the heavy wooden doors. Inside the front lobby, Trevor Jones, the head custodian, is pushing a broom across the gleaming tiles. Trevor is one of the true links between the regular school year and the imaginary one we create in the summer-time. He keeps the building humming along. He can often be found hanging out around the set, watching scenes play out. He's even been on-screen several times, when they needed some background action. He basically plays himself.

"Morning, Trevor," I say as I stroll past him.

"How's it going, Aiden? You making a pit stop at craft services?"

"As if you need to ask," I say with a wink.

He laughs as I continue down the hallway. Trevor is used to me arriving early on set, and although it's true that I'm needed in wardrobe soon, I still have a little time. The real reason I like to show up early is because of craft services.

There are a lot of perks to being on a TV show, but at the top of my list is craft services, the department responsible for making sure that the cast and crew are never hungry between meals. Craft, as it's generally known, is separate from catering, which handles actual meals. From the moment I stepped onto my first set, I was in love with craft services. An entire department devoted to providing me with delicious snacks. I still wonder sometimes what the catch is.

I follow my nose down the central hallway to production central. I'm one of the first people on set, other than some carpenters dismantling the kitchen set from last week and starting to pull together what looks like a doctor's office. Chill Bill's desk on the stage is empty.

I beeline across the shiny wooden floor to Jenny, who runs craft services. She's preparing stacks of breakfast sandwiches and wrapping them in little tinfoil packages for the cast and crew, who will be arriving—hungry—any time.

"Morning, Jenny," I say as my eyes dance across the table of chocolates, candies and various types of chips and nachos.

She turns around from her little two-burner hot plate and smiles.

"You're just in time, Aiden," she says. "Fresh off the grill." She slides a steaming-hot breakfast sandwich into a tinfoil bag and passes it to me. The fragrant smell of bacon makes my mouth water.

"You're a saint, Jenny." I step out of the way as a gang of hungry set decorators walks up, looking for a fix. I grab a paper plate and round out my breakfast with a handful of Doritos, a few mini chocolate bars and my favorite—gummy worms. Then I head out to find someplace quiet to stuff my face and go over my scenes for the day.

I push through a door into one of the side hallways and make my way to one of my go-to hiding places, a little alcove where a vending machine hums quietly. I unsling my backpack and dig around for my script, then wedge myself into the space beside the pop machine. There's usually so much activity on set that I find it really hard to focus on learning my lines, so I like to hide away for a while before I shoot a scene. I'm always amazed at Satri, who can eat a burger while carrying on a conversation and only seems to need a few quick glances at his script. He never misses a line and is really good at improv too. Don't get me wrong, I think I'm pretty good, but I wish it came naturally to me like it does to Satri.

I balance the script on my knees. I let the paper plate nestle down in the V between my legs and my belly. I flip to the right page in the script, take a deep whiff of my sandwich, then begin to happily chow down while scanning my lines.

I'm only halfway through my sandwich when I hear a door bang open. Footsteps echo down the hallway and stop about ten feet from where I'm sitting.

"I just don't understand how this is coming up out of nowhere!" I recognize the voice right away. Chill Bill. Although he doesn't sound so chill at the moment.

"Bill, you need to relax," says a second voice, this one calmer but more businesslike. Not as familiar, but I'm pretty sure it's Barbara Kale, the producer of *Pop Quiz*. I've never really been clear on what a producer does exactly, but I know Barbara only comes to the set once in a while. I think she's responsible for money and TV networks and contracts and stuff, while Bill is responsible for what happens on-screen.

"I'm sorry, Bill," she continues, "but the budget just isn't adding up. And ratings have been going down for a while now. Traditional TV is dead, Bill. You know that as well as anyone. Everyone is getting their entertainment online. I'm telling you this now so you have time to figure out how to tell the cast."

"Tell the cast?" asks Bill. "You mean you expect *me* to deliver this news?"

"Bill, come on," Barbara says. "You know that they all trust you, and like you."

"And you think they'll feel that way after this?" he asks.

A cell phone rings, and for a moment they are silent as someone rummages for a phone. "I have to get this," says Barbara. "We'll finish this conversation later, Bill." I hear the click-clack of heels and a door shutting. The hallway is silent once more.

I wait a second, wondering what to do, then stick my head around the side of the alcove. Bill is standing against the wall, and he's slowly rubbing his head.

"Bill?" I'm not sure if I should say anything.

He turns to me, surprised. "What are you doing here, Aiden?" he asks.

I hold out my script and wave it. "Running lines," I say.

He nods. "Good," he says dazedly. "You're a hard worker, buddy. That'll get you places."

"Is everything okay?" I ask.

"What? Oh, yeah. Yeah, things are fine." He turns as if he's going to head back to the room he came from, then spins on his heel. "I've gotta go, Aiden," he says. "I have some things to take care of before we get rolling today."

"Sure, Bill," I say. But he doesn't seem to hear me. He's already walking down the hallway and quickly disappears around a corner.